THE MOON OVER WAPAKONETA

FICTIONS AND SCIENCE FICTIONS FROM INDIANA AND BEYOND

MICHAEL MARTONE

FC2

TUSCALOOSA

FC2 is an imprint of The University of Alabama Press
Inquiries about reproducing material from this work should be addressed to
The University of Alabama Press

Book Design: Publications Unit, Department of English, Illinois State
    University; Director: Steve Halle, Production Assistant: Charley Koenig
Cover Design: Lou Robinson
Typeface: Adobe Garamond Pro

Library of Congress Cataloging-in-Publication Data
Names: Martone, Michael author.
Title: The moon over Wapakoneta : fictions & science fictions from Indiana
& beyond / Michael Martone.
Description: Tuscaloosa : FC2, 2018. | Includes bibliographical references. |
Identifiers: LCCN 2018006878 (print) | LCCN 2018011516 (ebook) |
ISBN
9781573668798 (Ebook) | ISBN 9781573660686 (pbk.)
Classification: LCC PS3563.A7414 (ebook) | LCC PS3563.A7414 A6
2018b (print)
| DDC 813/.54—dc23
LC record available at https://lccn.loc.gov/2018006878

FOR SAM & NICK
THE WILD. THE BLUE. THE YONDER.

CONTENTS

THE MOON OVER WAPAKONETA

THE MOON OVER WAPAKONETA

1.

There is the moon, full, over Wapakoneta, Ohio. Everybody I know has a sister or a brother, a cousin or an uncle living up there now. The moon is studded green in splotches, spots where the new atmospheres have stuck, mold on a marble.

2.

I'm drunk. I'm always drunk. Sitting in the dust of a field outside Wapakoneta, Ohio, I look up at the moon. The moon, obscured for a moment by a passing flock of migratory satellites flowing south in a dense black stream, has a halo pasted behind it. That meant something once, didn't it?

3.

When the moon is like it is now, hanging over Ohio, I come over to Wapakoneta from Indiana where I am from. I am legal in Ohio, and the near beer they can sell to minors is so near to the real thing it is the real thing. I told you I was drunk. The foam head of this beer glows white in the dull light like the white rubble of the moon bearing down from above. Over there, somewhere, is Indiana, a stone's throw away.

4.

Everybody I know has a brother or cousin or whoever on the moon, and I am using this pilsner for a telescope. Where is everybody? The old craters are percolating. They've been busy as bees up there. Every night a new green explosion, another detonation of air. This is where I make myself belch.

5.

The reflection of the moon over Wapakoneta sinks into each flat black solar panel of this field where I sit, a stone swallowed by a pond. In the fields, the collectors pivot slowly, tracking even the paler light of the moon across the black sky. There's this buzz. Cicada? Crickets? No. voltage chirps, generated as the moon's weak light licks the sheets of glass.

6.

Let's power up my personal downlink. Where am I?—I ask by nudging the ergonomic toggle. Above me, but beneath the moon over Ohio, a satellite, then, perhaps, another peels away from its flock to answer my call. Let's leave it on. More satellites will cock their heads above my head, triangulating till the cows come home. But soft, the first report is in. Ohio, the dots spell out, Wapakoneta.

7.

What part of the moon is the backwater part? Maybe there, that green expanse inches from the edge where they are doing battle with the airless void generating atmosphere from some wrangling of biomass. Yeah, back there under the swirl of those new clouds, some kid after a hard day of—what?—making cheese, lies on his back and has a smoke consuming a mole of precious oxygen. He looks up at the earth through the whiffs of cloud and smoke and imagines some Podunk place where the slack-jawed inhabitants can't begin to imagine being pioneers, being heroes. There it is, Ohio.

8.

A pod of jalopies takes off from the pad of Mr. Entertainer's parking lot, racing back to Indiana where it's an hour earlier. The road is lined with Styrofoam crosses, white in the moonlight, and plastic flowers oxidized by the sunlight. X marks the spot where some hopped-up Hoosier goes airborne for a sec and then in a stupor remembers gravity and noses over into the ditch next to a field outside of Wapakoneta on the trailing edge of Ohio.

9.

They are launching their own satellites from the moon; a couple of dozen a day the paper says. Cheap in the negative gees. Gee. I look hard at the moon. I want to see the moons of the moon. The moon and its moons mooning me. In Ohio, I pull my pants down and moon the moon and its moons mooning me back. And then, I piss. I piss on the ground, my piss falling, falling to earth, falling to the earth lit up by the moon, my piss falling at the speed of light to the ground.

10.

I am on the move. I am moving. Drawn by the gravitational pull of Mr. Entertainer with its rings of neon, I am steering a course by the stars. Better check in. More of the little buzz bombs have taken up station above my head. Surprise! I am in Wapakoneta. I am in Wapakoneta, but I am moving. I am moving within the limits of Wapakoneta. I like to make all the numbers dance, the dots on the screen rearranging. X, Y, and Z, each axis scrolling, like snow in a snow dome. The solar panels in the field around me slowly track the moon as it moves through the night sky.

11.

Over there in Indiana, it's an hour earlier. Don't ask me why. You cross a road, State Line Road, and you step back in time. It can be done. Heading home, I get this gift, an extra hour to waste. But wait! I lost one someplace coming here. I shed it when I crossed the street, like sloughing skin. It must be somewhere, here at my feet. This pebble I nudge with my toe. Just what time is it? I consult my other wrist where the watch burbles, all its dials spinning, glowing softly, little moon. The laser beam it emits ricochets off my belt buckle, noses up to find its own string of satellites, bouncing around a bit, kicking the can, homing for home, an atomic clock on a mountaintop out west to check in on each millisecond of the passing parade, then, in a blink, it finds its way back to me here, makes a little beep. Beep! Here's the report: Closing Time.

12.

Mr. Entertainer is not very entertaining. It's powering down before my eyes, each neon sign flickers, sputters in each dark window. The whole advertised universe collapsing in on the extinguished constellation of letters. How the hell did that happen. I had my eye on things, and the moon over Wapakoneta hasn't moved as far as I can tell. The rubble of the bar is illuminated now by that soft indifferent dusty light diffused through the dust kicked up by the departed cars. The slabs of its walls fall into blue shadow; its edges, then, drift into a nebulous fuzz, a cloud floating just above the ground.

13.

What time is it on the moon? It's noon there now. It's noon on the moon. From the stoop of the extinct bar, I consider the moon's midday that lasts for days, lunch everlasting, amen. They must get drunk on the light. They must drink it up. They must have plenty to spare. The excess is spilling on me, pouring on me down here in Ohio, enough light for me, a heavenly body, to cast a shadow on the studded gravel galaxy of the empty parking lot, a kind of time piece myself, the armature of an impromptu moon dial, the time ticking off as my celestial outline creeps from one cold stone to the next.

14.

Cars on the road are racing back to Indiana. I hear them dribbling the sound of their horns in front of them, leaking a smear of radio static in the exhaust. I am looking for my clunker. It's around here someplace. According to my uplink, I am still in Wapakoneta. A slow night for the satellites, they have been lining up to affirm that consensus, a baker's dozen have been cooking up coordinates. I punch a button on my car key releasing the ultrasonic hounds hot on the magnetic signature of my piece of shit. The nearby solar panels pivot toward me sensing the valence of my reflection, hunger for the light I am emitting. Hark! Somewhere in the vast relative dark the yodel of a treed automobile. I must calculate the vectors for my approach.

15.

Later, in Indiana, which is now earlier, I will remember back to this time, this time that is happening now, as I navigate by means of sonic boom to the bleat of my Mother Ship supposedly fastened to the edge of some solar panel field out there somewhere in the dark. But the sound is reverberating, gone doppler, bouncing off the copse of antennae to the right, the bank of blooming TV dishes to the left. The night air has become acoustic, dampening the reports. I am getting mixed signals, and it seems my car is moving around me. That may be the case. Perhaps I left it in autopilot. It's nosing toward home this very minute, sniffing the buried wire, or, perhaps it's just playing games with me, its own guidance system on some feedback loop, as it orbits under the influence of an ancient cruising pattern programmed long ago for the high school drag in Fort Wayne. My guardian satellites, whispering to each other, hover above my head, shaking theirs, "Lost, poor soul, in Ohio, in the holy city of Wapakoneta."

16.

Everybody I know has a sister or a brother, a mom or a dad setting up housekeeping in some low rent crater of the moon. I intercept postcards—low gain transmissions of the half of earth in the black sky and a digital tweet eeping "Wish You Were Here!"—when I eavesdrop on the neighborhood's mail. On nights like this, with the moon radiating a whole spectrum of sunny missives, I want to broadcast a wide band of my own billet-doux banged out with a stick on any handy piece of corrugated steel in the ancient language of killing time.

17.

I fall into the ditch or what I think is the ditch. Flat on my back, I stare up at the moon, canvas, sailing above this pleasant seat, my bishopric, and find myself thinking of my kith and kin again and again. The starlight scope is in the car. I hear its honk still, a goose somewhere in the marsh night asking the tower for permission to land. If I had the goggles now, I could see where

I've landed but would, more likely, be blinded by this moon-light boosted by the sensitive optics. Night would be day, and the moon over Wapakoneta would be more like the sun over Wapakoneta. I might see some real sun soon if I just close my unaided eyes for a bit and let the whole Ptolemaic contraption overhead wheel and deal.

18.

But the watch I wear is still turned on and on the lookout for pulses of light angling back this way from the fibrillating iso-topes atop Pikes Peak. The watch's microprinted works synthesize a "bleep" a second, a steady erosion to my will to doze. At the top of each hour, it drops a drip, and this absence more than the regular tolling pricks me to a semiconducted alertness. The solar panels at the lip of the ditch chirp their chirp, Wapakoneta's moon, a dilated pupil centered in each dark iris. And there's the car's snarled sound still hoping to be found. So much for silent night, holy night. Lo, a rocket off yonder rips the raw cloth of night.

19.

At that moment I open my eyes, and in the ditch with me is the big ol' moon its ownself half buried in the mud. Hold on there! There is the moon, the moon over Wapakoneta. It's there up above, where it should be. It's there over this other moon mired in the mud of Wapakoneta. My eyes adjust to the light. O! I'm not in the ditch but on the berm below the old moon museum, the building's geodesic concrete dome, teed up on a dimple in a hummock in Ohio, mocking the moon overhead. The real moon rises above the arching horizon of this fallen fake.

20.

Armstrong hailed from these Wapakonetish parts. Got drunk here on near beer, I suppose. Contemplated the strobing codes of lightning bugs down by the river. The river caught the moon's pale and silent reflection Pitched a little woo, too. Looked up at the moon, very same moon I spy with my little eye. First guy to go there. Got a pile of rocks marking the spot there. I've seen pictures. "Wish you were here!" Down here, they keep the moon rocks he brought back under glass in the hollowed-out moon building before me. The school kids, on field trips, herd by the cases of rocks. The little rocks. The big rocks. Big deal! The kids have got a brother or sister, uncles and aunts, sweeping the dust together into neat piles upstairs. Here's to the first man on the moon from the last person on earth.

21.

The earth is slowing down. Friction as it twirls. When the moon untucks the oceans, makes the tides bulge, it's like holding your hand out the car window as you race toward Indiana, a drag against the cool night air, skidding to a halt. Long time coming. Every once in awhile, they throw in a leap second or two to bring the world back up to speed. Another cipher of silence at the top of the hour to keep the whole thing in tune. One day the earth will creep to a crawl, and one side will always be facing the face of the moon always facing me. A slow spinning dance around the sun. My watch skips a beat. The silence stretches on and on.

22.

At twelve o'clock high, a huge flock of satellites floats in formation, veiling the moon. They are migrating north. The swallows returning to Capistrano. A new season? Reconnoitering to be done by morning? Who knows. My own orbiting dovecot coos to me still, homing, homing. You are in Ohio, in Wapakoneta, in Ohio. I release them just like that. The blank LED goes white in the moonlight. They disperse, disappear, kids playing hide and seek in the dark.

23.

At my feet are rocks painted blue by the moon's light. I pick one up out of the dust and launch it into space at the moon hanging over Ohio. I lose sight of it, swallowed up in the intense glare I am aiming at. Sure thing! I've chucked it beyond the bounds of earth. It's slipped into space on the grease of its own inertia. But I hear its reentry, splashing into the ocean of solar panels yards away, the light we've all been staring at turning solid. I heave another sputnik into orbit, hoping to even up the gross mass of the planets which is all out of whack in this binary system. I'm a run-of-the-mill vandal, my slight buzz waning. But soft! A frog jumps into a pond. It makes that sound a frog makes when it jumps into a pond.

24.

Didn't I tell you? It is an hour earlier in Indiana. The moon over Wapakoneta is gaining on me here as I race along the section roads toward home, all of its imaginable phases caught by the thousands and thousands of black reflections in their tropic glass panels. The moon waxes on all the mirrored surfaces, silent, a skipping stone skipping. Yes, I'll catch it tonight as it sets, embrace it, a burned-out pebble, in my empty backyard.

THE DIGITALLY ENHANCED IMAGE OF CARY GRANT[1] APPEARS IN A CORNFIELD IN INDIANA[2]

In September, Benjamin Day, his wife, Irene, and their two sons, Norbert and August, witnessed the miraculous and seemingly spontaneous appearance of the actor Cary Grant (in his role as Roger Thornhill in Hitchcock's *North by Northwest*[3]) in the opposite oncoming unpaved shoulder of US Route 41 at Prairie, a rural Greyhound bus stop, near Ade, Indiana, halfway between Chicago and Indianapolis. The bewildered apparition responded (as the Days, on the way to Irene's sister's place in Kentland, pulled over to park) with a look of anxious anticipation as if he (Cary Grant[4]) had perhaps come to this spot to rendezvous with a person or persons unknown to him at this otherwise deserted

---

1. Cary Grant was born Archibald Leach on 18 January 1904 in Bristol, England, to an overly possessive mother and distant father.
2. It was admitted as the 19th state in 1816. The area was controlled by France until 1763 and then by Great Britain until 1783. Population 5,490,260. Or a borough of west-central Pennsylvania, east-northeast of Pittsburgh.
3. Originally known as *The Man in Lincoln's Nose*, *North by Northwest* came by its official title from *Hamlet*: "I am mad north-north-west."
4. For the rest of his life, he felt that his insecurity with women, his desire to control them, stemmed in large measure from being led to believe that his mother had abandoned him.

location (the very situation portrayed in the movie). Cary Grant[5] (who the Days had recognized only from his performances in movies and mainly then when replayed on television) flickered on the side of the road, the pattern[6] of his tailored suit[7] strobing in the bright sunlight. Seemingly vexed and appearing to be searching for words, the actor (who the Days believed had been dead for years[8]) undid the button on his jacket and, squinting, looked both north and south, scanning for traffic before beginning to cross the empty highway approaching the Days' automobile in a rather sheepish manner. "Hi," it (or he) said. "Hot day." Mr. Day responded with, "Seen worse." There was a long uncomfortable silence during which the solid projected image of the screen actor wavered and seemed to dissipate. Through the translucent chest of the tongue-tied matinee idol, the Days now noted an emerging insect-like speck on the horizon of what would become the menacing crop-dusting biplane[9] growing larger as it a) approached or b) became visually enriched by continuing production of escaped free radical holographic microwave carrier pixel transmissions or c) grew in the mass pixilated mind of the hysterical family Day

---

5. He had been offered many millions to write his autobiography. He refused, saying he didn't want to embarrass anyone, including himself.

6. Glen plaid checks, originally known as Glenurquhart checks. Glen plaid sometimes referred to as "Prince of Wales" checks was initially woven of saxony wool and was later found in tweed, cheviot, plied, and worsted cloth.

7. Brooks Brothers introduced the No. 1 sack suit in 1895. Designed to fit all body types, the suit offered soft natural shoulders, a single-breasted jacket, and full, plain-front trousers.

8. 11:22pm, 29 November 1986. Massive stroke. While visiting Davenport, Iowa, with his "Conversation" show.

9. The single-engined Stearman biplane was originally designed as a simple, sturdy, military two-seater trainer. The history of agricultural aviation dates back to 1917 when a cotton field in Louisiana was dusted.

seriously affected by a hallucinogenic toxin produced by secretions from mold spores present on the rye bread of their recently consumed ham sandwiches or d) became another (along with the miraculous image of Cary Grant) actual blessed mystery of The Lord God Almighty. The ultimate of the above list of options chosen by the Days (devout Roman Catholics) themselves during their recovery and currently under investigation by the Diocese of Fort Wayne/South Bend as an actual miracle attributed to the intercession of the Beatified Wendell Willkie and commemorated by a small shrine on the spot and its inclusion in the officially sanctioned pilgrimage of St. James of the Starry Fields. "Are you supposed to be meeting someone here?" the resolidified image of Cary Grant asked the inanimate Days who then (as if on cue) shook their heads *no* in unison. "Oh, then ah, then your name isn't Kaplan?" At this point the details of the event in the Days' retelling become somewhat sketchy. But there is a transition of some kind as the distant airplane[10] on the horizon metastasizes above their heads, leading to the reenactment of the celebrated chase of Cary Grant by the aforementioned crop-dusting biplane[11] through a cornfield[12] in Indiana. On the first pass, Grant falls down onto the dirt[13] covering his head as the plane swoops

---

10. The aircraft is flown with a constant throttle, the pilot regulating the altitude with the stick. If the aeroplane is equipped with an adjustable propeller, this is kept in course pitch. Longitudinal trim is mostly set in neutral. Some pilots prefer a slight nose-up setting, which give additional safety in the event of striking birds or other incidents.

11. It is evident that prolonged low altitude flying puts a severe strain upon the pilot and calls for very special qualities.

12. A polystichous diploid with unisex inflorescences and rigid rachilla.

13. Alluvium: soil deposited by water such as a flowing river. Duff: soil found on the forest floor, leaf litter and other organic debris in various stages

low then running again only to collapse once more into a "shallow depression" as the overtaking plane unleashes a barrage of automated[14] weapons[15] fire (the end result of which is the eruption of soil all around the prostrate and vaporous Cary Grant spraying him with the resulting vaporized dirt). Scrambling up from the ground, Grant then runs back to the highway to flag down an approaching car that passes through him without slowing down. He turns and runs (and falls), pursued by the rapidly accelerating, diving biplane into a stand of dried corn[16] (brittle in the wind kicked up by strafing plane flying a few feet above the tasseled stalks). The plane circles for another pass, this time emitting contrails of aerially applied insecticide[17] on Cary Grant's suspected location in the rows of corn. The cloud of descending poison[18]

---

of decay. Eluvium: soil and mineral particles blown and deposited by the wind. Gumbo: fine silty soil known for its sticky mud. Loam: soil consisting of sand, clay, silt, and organic matter. Mull: an upper mineral layer mixed with organic matter.

14. An automatic weapon is one in which the process of feeding, firing, extracting, and ejecting is carried out by the mechanism of the weapon after a primary manual, electric, or pneumatic cocking as long as the trigger is held and the supply of ammunition in the belt, feed strip, or magazine lasts.

15. These weapons embodied simple blowback actions and were chambered for cartridges from caliber .45 to 9mm with magazine capacities of 25–32 rounds and operated in cyclic rates of 500–600 rounds per minute at a maximum effective range of 200 yards.

16. Corn demands a quantity of water because it sweats, or "transpires" heavily. A full-grown plant on a hot July day in an Iowa cornfield will transpire five to nineteen pounds of water, while an acre of plants will transpire 720 tons.

17. DDT is an abbreviation derived from the common name d(ichloro) d(iphenyl)t(richloroethane). The proper name for the insecticidal compound is 1,1,1, tricloro-2,2bis(parachlorophenyl)etane.

blankets him (a ghost in a ghostly cloud). He reaches for a handkerchief and covers his mouth and nose. Flushed and flushed from hiding, Grant breaks back into the open, heading for the highway once again (where in the movie a fuel tanker truck will run him over and then said truck receives in a fiery crash the too closely pursuing menacing aircraft). But then Cary Grant just disappears in mid stride as the Days gape (their memories of the event expired or their memory of the movie incomplete). The airplane (too) vanishes. "But what has really happened?" the narrator intones. The Days of Ade, Indiana, have told their story to a variety of interested governmental, religious, academic, and media entities whose representatives descended upon this part of Indiana like flights of menacing crop-dusting biplanes. The recounting of events has now been transcribed and archived (as well) assuring that the next appearance of Cary Grant in Indiana will be all the more complete (approaching perfection in its exactness, in its subsequent reiterations), looped (as it were) back into this place (the focal point of a few feet of framed film) this place that (most will tell you) wasn't on the map (perhaps), never really existed before the movie (*North by Northwest*) was produced and shown and brought this tiny sacred (what?) precinct (stuttering) to a kind of life...

---

18. The storage of DDT on human fat is a consequence of its differential solubility. DDT is almost completely insoluble in water but much more soluble in nonpolar solvents including lipid tissue.

THE MAN'S WATCH

1. She was already naked except for the man's watch she wore on her right wrist.

2. She didn't take the watch off as she watched him undress.

3. Because the watch was on her right hand, she used her left to rub herself, watching as he undressed.

4. Moving, inside her, on top of her, he watched the watch.

5. It was a man's watch with a flat wafer-thin face, silver Italian design, twelve black Arabic numbers, and black leather band.

6. Her arms were thrown up over her head, and she had twisted the watch's band so the face rested on the inside of her wrist.

7. As they moved together, he watched the watch.

8. The watch had a sweep second hand as thin as a hair, and he was conscious that he was timing himself and keeping track of how long it all was taking.

9. As she came, he counted the seconds she took, watching the watch as it pulsed on her wrist.

10. Then, as he came, he noted the time, how the minute hand and the hour hand on the watch had traded places, how at some time while they made love the one hand had slipped over the other hand, changing slightly the angle the two hands formed, the look of the tiny black wedge hovering over the silver, a sliver less than or more than.

11. Afterward, still in bed he said something about the watch, was it new and how unusual it had been for her to keep it on when she undressed.

12. Right then she gave him the watch, taking it off and giving it to him.

13. It's a man's watch, she said, and when I saw it in the store I thought of you.

14. They had been meeting this way for twelve years, the number of numbers on the watch.

15. He didn't wear the man's watch home but hid it in his luggage, and when he got home he left the watch hidden there in his unpacked luggage.

16. He had never worn a watch, had always asked the time or remembered where the clocks were, glancing at them without thinking, to get the sense of the time, of time passing.

17. If he started wearing the man's watch its appearance would have to be explained.

18. He took the watch with him every time he traveled, wearing it only while he was on the road.

19. On the road, he got used to wearing the watch and would think of her and the time she gave it to him every time he looked at the watch.

20. At night, from hotel rooms, he would leave messages for her, telling her how he loved the watch she had given him, how he was looking at it right now, reading the time passing, spending his anytime minutes.

21. Later, he lost the watch in a hotel room.

22. Time went by, and he didn't tell her he had lost the watch but lied when he talked to her on the phone.

23. He searched stores and catalogues for an identical watch to replace the one he had lost.

24. He was afraid to see her again without the watch she had given him, and he hoped to see her again soon.

25. At last he found a watch that matched his lost watch offered by a company online, and he ordered it right away.

26. The watch came.

27. But now that he had the watch again, he never saw her again.

28. The rendezvous when she had given him the watch had been the last time they would see each other, and he hadn't known it until, much later, when, with a telephone message, she told him she couldn't do this anymore.

29. He thought of the twists of old O. Henry stories, the ones with watches and exchanges of gifts.

30. Once, a long time ago, before the watch, naked in bed after making love, they had talked about their lives and their life together.

31. She believed that there were many moments in each life when that life changed utterly, irrevocably, a tick of a watch's second hand and everything was, is, will be different.

32. He believed in the accumulation of events, no dramatic reversals but the slow shearing away of countless seconds as the watch's minute hand and its hour hand opened and closed, cutouts of lacy paper hearts or intricate doily snowflakes.

33. He thought then of the atomic clock and its accuracy so fine that from time to time it had to add a leap second to compensate for the slowing of the earth by friction and how the extra second was broadcast to all those new-fangled watches and clocks so equipped for receiving the signal to pause.

34. He wasn't wearing the watch when he listened to her message, the one that said she couldn't do this anymore.

35. Even though he wasn't wearing the watch when he listened to the message, he knew the exact moment when it happened.

36. His voice mail had its own internal clock, and a digital voice made to sound like a woman's voice told him the exact time the message had been received.

37. A long time ago, when they made love while she was wearing the watch, it seemed to last forever.

38. But that was an illusion that the watch dispelled.

39. He remembers counting the seconds as she came, a handful of seconds.

40. And his own orgasm took even less time, the watch's second hand leaping from one jeweled hash mark to the next.

41. The earth moved not in any dramatic way but in its everyday everyday way, the watch marking this just perceptible torque.

42. And afterward, the watch didn't stop but proceeded to the next lost moment and the next.

43. He wished now that he hadn't been distracted by the machinations of the watch, as he knew now that that had been the last time he would be with her.

44. His memory had been set by watching the watch's face and not her face.

45. And later he asked her about the watch, and right there on the spot she started to take off the watch, unstrapping it from her wrist.

46. It is a man's watch, she said, when I saw the watch I thought of you.

47. He watched her take the watch from her wrist.

48. She was naked except for the watch, and when she took off the watch she seemed even more naked.

49. And soon after giving him the watch she began to dress, putting her rings on last as she had always done before.

50. And in the time since then they talked on the phone many times about the watch, about the last time they had seen each other, and about the next time they would see each other.

51. After he lost the watch, searching for the watch, he looked at hundreds of watches.

52. When he found the watch he thought was the watch she had given him and he had lost, he hoped it would be the same watch but it wasn't of course.

53. The new watch was like the old watch but it was different.

54. Then, one day, after he had lost the watch and bought its replica, he got a message from her saying she couldn't do this anymore.

55. He played the message over and over, timing its duration with the watch he had taken from hiding.

56. Looking at the watch while listening to her voice, he wanted to turn back time or, at the very least, find a way to suspend time, to stop it, to slow it, at least.

57. The watch wouldn't let him do it.

58. The watch she had given to him, he gave to his wife.

59. It's a man's watch, she said, putting it on.

60. She was already naked except for the man's watch she wore on her right wrist.

ANTON CHEKHOV WRITES TO HIS FRIEND, WILLIAM SYDNEY PORTER, IN THE COLUMBUS, OHIO, FEDERAL PENITENTIARY

My Dear Porter,

I write to you from my own prison, my hothouse Siberia, Yalta. Olga has already returned to the city. By all means, I will be married if you wish it. But on these conditions: everything must be as it has been hitherto—that is, she must live in Moscow while I live in the country, and I will come to see her. Oh give me a wife who, like the moon, won't appear in my sky every day. Here the work is hard, and I write with much difficulty. I long for the days before the consumption and before I turned inward, generally, thinking myself the artist, before that, when I wrote serenely, the way I eat pancakes now. It is the oppressive heat of these environs that has informed my mood, made me moody, propels me to create, in this theater, a theater of mood. Nothing happens here and yet everything does. There, it happened there, right there at the "yet," the fulcrum of the previous sentence, when things, *things*, turned. Turned inside out. Turned outside in. The secret, we know, is the animation of that thing called "nothing," its locomotion. Like that actual engine, which moves and at the same time moves. The whole contrivance propelled forward while the mechanism of movement—the driving wheels, the pistons and rods, their hubs and bearings—furiously spins. So our texts move and move. The plot on its rails hems and haws while the clockwork of character, the true motive power, the underlying organic lubrication for such incremental perturbation, supplies the real leverage, the play in the works. I think of you, my dear Porter, there in the hospital wing of your prison mixing potions. Incarcerated, proscribed from action, you, trustee, still live, do you not? Inside, you are inside. Inside, you are forced upon your inner resources. Penitent. And I, stewing here in my Yalta, stew too. My doctors tell me both my lungs are now fully involved. I have, Sydneyvitch, a very active inner life. That is a joke, a joke. My silences? No longer silent. Hear that rattle in my breathing? The express train, a stutter of steel wheels over the joints in the steel rails. We see these things differently, you and I. As a druggist you find the world all chemistry. The reagents and reactants in your reactions acting predictable, your doses dose, and do-see-do. As a doctor, I think, what more is there for me to do now—now that we have stopped the bloodletting, returned the leeches back to the wild—but, after a careful read of the symptoms, to diagnose. And then, after that, to sit, to wait and see how it all comes out. How it all comes out. Before you are your mortar and pestle. The ingredients, atomized and combined, a direct result of the pressures of your own hand, your eye for measurement, the proven formulas. Here, there is my patient, taking the airs on the boardwalk with his family, oblivious, the grape clusters of alveoli in his lungs mildewing as he speaks, more rusty with each breath until when one day... My dear Porter, one day you must settle on a name. It is not difficult to follow you through the pages of *McClure's*, as your distinctive stories and style are your signature even as you disguise yourself from yourself name after name. It is perhaps our greatest work, our most telling character, the one we construct for our own inhabitation. Our fictions are mere fashion, our wardrobe, even when tailored without prison stripes. Our work a kind of portable prison, Monsieur Porter. We all come from beneath the overcoat, my friend. Imagine there in your many prisons, your prisons inside prisons, a final name, a finished character, the world can alter with a proper suffix, ironic, surprising in a good way, something to hang an -esque onto.

I remain yours, etc.

Antasha

SEVEN FLAG DAYS

1. When I was a kid, in geometry class, no less with my lined
    paper ruled by rectangles, I taught myself to doodle a wav-
    ing flag, snapping the top and bottom lines into a cursive
    C, convex above and concave below, hooking up the humps
    with the paralleling lines that traced this new wrinkled
    wrinkle. It almost snapped. I shaded it as well, darkening
    the chiaroscuro of the deeply scored folds and filling in the
    space with similarly distorted stripes, the red ones the color
    of the silvery pencil lead, the white ones the white of the
    paper underneath, cheating, uncolored. I could make it
    look as if it was rippling, adding another lesser S, lesser S's.
    It was plain geometry, but I could add this third dimension.
    How was one to calculate the area of this? Area in motion.
    It was as if I were making cloth out of whole cloth, adding
    inches to the fly as it flew. Behind it, in what was now the
    depth of the page, I placed a few harmless clouds on the far
    horizon line that were only interrupted by stands of numer-
    ical figures and neighborhoods of letters, and all the rect-
    angles unfurled, nudged open by the dulling pencil point to
    the point that it began to smear. I drew the staffs that bleed

off the bottom of the page and improvised pennants and ensigns to fill the empty pages and overlapped one flag with another until the sheet of paper was scaled, a chain mail of flags shielding the problems from view, impossible now to prove or even imagined ever being posed.

2. My office is in the basement of the capitol, not far from the room beneath the rotunda where the Lincoln catafalque is kept in storage, in what was to have been Washington's tomb had the family let George and Martha be moved from Mount Vernon. I work for the Architect of the Capitol and it's a full-time job for me but not for the Architect of the Capitol who has other things to do and other people to do them with. I have two big cabinets in here—one for the Democrats and one for the Republicans. I am to keep the flags separate. I keep them separate though when they fly over the Capitol they fly in the same air. I have a detachment of marines who help—a couple dozen PFCs and lance corporals with a gunnery sergeant and a lieutenant fresh from Annapolis in command. When it rains, the Marines crowd around the big table, where the calligraphers inscribe the certificates, playing finger football for money, flicking those folded paper triangles with their fingers through the finger goalposts of the fellow's across the table. I never know the uniform of the day. Blue dress. Blue white dress. Reds and whites and several kinds of blues. And green blouses with their service dress, sometimes with garrison cap piss cutter covers and matt finished badges of the eagles, globes, and anchors. And other times in camouflaged utilities, the camouflage made up of tiny digitally designed dots and

dashes. They smell of naphtha, neat's-foot oil on the leather, fruity fabric softener, and Old Bay seasoning from the soft-shell crabs they ate for lunch. I like it best when they wear the white gloves. The soft cloth handling the new cloth of the flags like the curators down in the museums on the mall.

3. The stars are embroidered and the stripes are individually sewn.

4. There are two flagpoles at the base of the dome on the East and West front of the capitol. Flags fly there, have flown there, day and night since the First World War. The other two flagpoles are on North and South wings and fly flags only when the chamber below is in session. The flag above the House of Representatives is raised and lowered by pages. My auxiliary flagpoles are to the west of the dome and invisible from the ground. There are a dozen of them, painted white with a brass ball on top. I can hear the dome flags popping and snapping in the brisk breeze. The empty clips on the halyards rattle against the metal poles, off-key, but in a scale that cobbles together a kind of melody, like rivets popping under pressure. The ropes whip around, a completely different sound from the rattle of the metal clips. I climb down from the little platform with its forest of tsk-ing flagpoles and walk across the graveled roof of the capitol. There at the edge I can see the mall with all the museums and galleries and the office buildings. The flags on each of the buildings are being raised, unfolding and coming to life as the invisible wind above the buildings takes hold. First one, then another, then the next. A

couple more. One, way down the mall, then one closer by. That flag sprinting up the pole, the hoist seamless and smooth, billows outward in one big rolling curl. Another taking its time, the flag hiccupping up the pole as if the rope is being hauled one handed. It is like watching flowers bloom. Or bombs explode, I suppose. Most are big flags. It takes seconds for the breeze to work through the cloth, find its way along the long rippling stripes and out the lufting ends. None I can see are frayed or frazzled. There in the far distance, the ground fog of flags at the foot of the Washington Monument looks, from here, like one ribbon ringing the stone. The breeze stiffens. Cirrus clouds skim over the Potomac out of the west curling in the severely clear blue sky above. The white facing of the dome above is still in shadow. I turn back to see Marines busy attaching the first wave of flags to the c-rings to start another busy day.

5. Staff sometimes, summer interns, school year or semester interns who like to ride the private subway from the office buildings, pages too, and now and then the actual constituent will show up with the Member at the door, the order in hand. A flag in memory of someone, a flag in honor of something. A veteran, say. Or a flag a veteran has requested for himself to drape his own casket. In some other office, in some other office building, somewhere in the District another bureaucrat like me makes his own arrangements with the soon-to-be-dead Navy and Marine vet who wants to be buried at sea. He's a kind of travel agent, connects the coffins with the outbound ship—frigates mostly but the lucky ones score carriers steaming from Norfolk—that dump

their lading on the lee side of the territorial waters line, sliding the body out from beneath the flag I authenticate here as having flown over the capitol, a strange sanctified final blanket. I get the orders from the Member, from the Senator, and I order the flags. An elementary school in Flagstaff, my favorite. A Moose lodge in Moose Lodge. Chambers of Commerce. Post Offices, City Halls, fire stations, art museums. Yacht Clubs, golf courses, shopping malls, hospitals. Flag stores. I have two big cabinets, lockers to hold the flags until they can be flown. One is for Republican Flags. The other holds Democratic ones. I sort the requests into two neat piles on my desk. There must be software for this. There most be software for the dead. Something. Something that keeps track of the bodies shipping out to sea or stacking up on the loading docks at Arlington or any of the national cemeteries anywhere. I just have to keep track of the bunting, the bundling blankets, a just-in-time delivery guarantee. I get the flags there in the nick of time, already aired out in the Capitol airspace. Who would know that this flag or this one had ever seen the light of day up there on the roof over my head? The few seconds it flaps fades the dye almost imperceptible as if someone could tell? I don't think so. It's some kind of magic trick, these pieces of cloth draped over a box or dyed cotton wrapping up, a raw linen-wrapped body. Now you see it. Now you don't.

6. The folding takes up the time. After the flag has been hauled down it takes awhile to make the thirteen folds, tuck the edges in, press the air out. The pillow of stars. The Marines take turns playing the roles of color guards and

flag bearer. They could do it in their sleep. They would tell you they don't race each other, the various squads hoisting flag after flag. Each squad hoists a flag then moves to the next pole while the first one unfurls and flies. Then hoists the second flag as a second squad hauls down the first and folds and, as the flag is folded, a third comes in to hoist a new flag and then moves on to haul down the flag on the next pole. Hoisting, hauling, folding, three squads of three working three poles and four platoons of squads working the dozen flagpoles. The folded bundles of stars tip over on the table as they begin to pile up, my clerks falling behind in the boxing, consulting the clipboards for which flag is which, keeping the Democratic flags separated from the Republican flags. Marines snap the folds into the lifeless flags. One. Two. The big long folds like the ones one would do for sheets and then the rapid eleven triangular tweaks the make this way and that with little huffs of breath. The elaborate hero sandwich of the flag. This goes on from dawn to dusk on a good day. We take rolling breaks for lunch so that even as a mess of them is eating a jumbo order of soft shell crabs, others continue hoisting the flags, hauling them down, and folding the stars into the envelopes made up of stripes.

7. In the sky, the jets on station circle the city. They vector in pairs down the Potomac and then up the Anacostia. I know there are other squadrons further out, beyond, deep in Virginia, out over the bay, sweeping through Delaware, Maryland, to the Pennsylvania line. There, the traffic helicopters hover and the jets fly cover—the President's flying

today. Airliners line up for approach to Reagan, each spaced and each one-step up stepped behind the other. And above Arlington, the air force is flying in formation, each hour on the hour, the missing man formation for the burials there. The odd plane out, peeling vertical, racing between the corduroy of contrails crisscrossing above him. He makes a loop to catch up with the wing over the ocean to head back to Andrews. Sparrows leap up in big blankets from feeding on scraps on the mall. There are pigeons and doves cruising the stone rafters and pediments looking for perches that haven't been sabotaged with nails and nets by the GSA. Ravens circle the turrets of the old castle, roost in the trees that are dying. The flags going up and coming down are like theatrical curtains, revealing, as they move, a formation of fighters or a lumbering cargo plane lifting skyward, the executive jets—the airborne limos en route outbound. The engine noise is constant, but I lose them behind the flags as they are passing. And most of the planes are carrying flags stored in the cockpits, held in the holds. I have seen the certificates that go out with those flags. The graphics are graphic. The guns blazing and the missiles launching, the airplane imposed on a sky of flag screened 40 percent, a sky saturated by flag. There, way above, banking all day, the glint of an AWACs that circles and spots all the traffic in the airspace, looking down on the chaos and directing the dance. Perhaps directing even those grackles circling the dome or that lone seagull hovering, hovering, attempting to touch down on the spiked eagle finial at the tip-top of the House's flagpole.

ALONZO REED, DICTATING TO HIS COLLABORATOR, BRAINERD KELLOGG, LOSES TRACK OF WHAT HE WAS THINKING ONLY TO NOTICE HIS AUDIENCE IS, ALREADY, LOST IN THOUGHT

"The fact that the pictorial diagram groups the parts of a sentence according to their offices and relations, and not in the order of speech, has been spoken of as a fault, but it is, on the contrary, a merit, for it teaches the pupil to look through the literary order and discover the logical order and learns what the literary order really is, and sees that this may be varied indefinitely so long as the logical relations are kept clear; the assertion that correct diagrams can be made mechanically is not borne out by the facts as it is easier to avoid precision in oral analysis than in written and the diagram drives the pupil to a most searching examination of the sentence, brings him face to face with every difficulty, and compels a decision on every point," he said, turning from the newly shattered window pane, the foul cricket ball, spent, nesting in the sward below, to study his collaborator, exhausted, sketch (stabbing really with his stubby forefinger), using the steam on the mirror above the buffet, a rudimentary experimental articulation of something he himself was just thinking, all the time thinking that this sentence the one he was thinking of now, the one he was beginning to reconstruct in his head, this sentence, even as it is unfinished to this point,

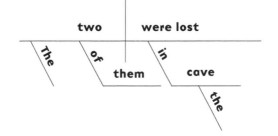

will, in fact, when it does finish, lend itself to their relentless and redundant methodology of vivisection, into these branching fractured fractions of speech, and he only worries that the one grammatical detour impossible to diagram will be the diagram itself diagramming the sentence—The two of them were lost in the cave—suspended there, a web inside a web, like the impossible pattern of switches, the frogs and points, found in the vast yards behind beneath around adjacent to Waterloo Station, including, within its web, the network of the Necropolis Railway, on its own timetable, dispatching as required, its three carriage trains of coffins and mourners, stuttering over the jointed rail, a kind of final punctuation, a code made up of these dashes and dots and the seemingly infinite spaces in between betweens.

A BUCKET OF WARM SPIT

Oncet, you could spit on the ground and grow water.

They said back then that the rain would follow the plow. They lied.

Our plows were painted grass green, and they broke open the green grass prairie hereabouts. Where it split and opened up, I swear, you could hear it leak, spitting a little spit, spit a hiss-like hiss.

Spit of steam here, spit of steam there, the ground a rolling boil, all that steam boiled up into a smoke of steam.

The water rained from the ground pouring into the sky sighing as it went. The water, it up and went.

After awhile all that water emptied into a big ol' cloud wall that hanged down from the sky and hugged the ground that feed it.

That big ol' cloud wall, it was made up of all these little drops of steam-water and seeded inside each of all these drops of steam-water were itty biddy grains of dust that got carried away, snug, that the water would stick to.

When that big ol' cloud begun to move with the big ol' wind a pushing it over the land, the grains of dust inside, they sanded the dry ground beneath it into more dust.

More more dust.

More dust got swallowed up by the dust and soon it was just dust in the big ol' cloud. That and a little paste of mud.

The land was wore away.

The land was wore away.

The land was turned into air. We breathed it in.

The land, it filled our lungs like food filled up a stomach but those were empty, our stomachs, even as we got to eating the dirt. We were eating dirt all the time as it up and went.

Jack, he kept burying his daddy.

Jack kept to burying his daddy in the dirt as it up and went.

Nobody farmed anymore. Nobody farmed.

We'd plow and the furrows would flatten. We'd plant and the seeds, they'd be blowed away. No need to hoe since the dirt-wind and the dirt-cloud scoured the ground clean of every weed.

Jack, he kept burying his daddy.

In that dirt-wind, Jack kept to burying his daddy.

Jack, he'd dig him a hole and roll his daddy, in his winding, into it.

The tailings Jack tossed into the hole turned to smoke on his shovel as he tossed them, trying to fill the hole he dug.

A whole spade full of soil smoking off the blade as he aimed for the hole with his daddy, in his winding, in it.

Jack, he'd end scooping the sandy sides of the hole over the sides of the hole to fill the hole up.

Jack, he dozed the dust with his feet, pushed the dust into hole to get it out of the wind, get the ground below ground out of the dirt-wind even as dirt-dirt washed away in the dirt-wind.

He'd finally get a blanket of that dirt-dirt over the body of his daddy, wrapped in the rotting winding.

Jack, he'd sit on top the dust he'd swept into the hole, but not to rest so much as to see if he could holt the dust down, keep it from drifting away again.

But the dust, it drifted away again.

He watched coils of dirt-dirt snake away from right under where he sat on it.

And Jack, he'd sink into the hole he dug as the dirt-dirt washed away from right under where he sat on it, wash away in the dirt-wind.

'Fore you know it, Jack, he would be all the way in the hole, sinking into it, with his daddy in his winding cloth. 'Cept there was no hole no more.

Jack, he'd stand back up and start to digging another hole to bury his daddy, his daddy in his rotting winding, lying in a heap on the shifting ground at his feet.

This went on a spell.

About then, the brindle cow, she run dry.

The brindle cow, she up and dried up.

Jack, he was in no ways surprised by this.

Jack, he'd been feeding the brindle cow wood from the barn, the red clapboards stripped of paint and sanded smooth by the dirt-wind.

Jack, he'd be back there massaging the bag to get the brindle cow to let down. The brindle cow, she'd be chewing and chewing the old barn wood all the time Jack was there in the back trying to get her to let down.

Jack, he'd work up a spit to spit on his hands to rub the boss's bag to get her to let down.

Before she give out, she'd give just one-half tin cup of rheumy cream.

To get that, Jack'd use all four teats for that one-half tin cup of rheumy cream the brindle cow would give after Jack'd massage her shrinking bag to get her to let down.

The brindle cow, she'd graze the sticking out tops of the buried bob-wire fences.

The fence pickets and the bob wire, they would knock the dirt-dust out of the wind and all get buried in the drift.

The brindle cow she would graze the fence tops, work the staples loose.

The brindle cow, she'd lick rust right off the bob wire. Her big ol' tongue licking the rust right off the wire.

Jack, he found himself one of them ol' magnets. He found one of them big ol' bar magnets and feed it to the brindle cow.

The ol' magnet, it is lodge up in the crop.

That ol' magnet up in the crop, it draws all the hardware the brindle cow grazed on.

That ol' magnet, it didn't do no good.

That ol' magnet, it didn't do no good at all cause the brindle cow went dry as a bone.

The brindle cow, she stopped all together letting down.

The brindle cow, she stopped all together letting down, stopped giving milk not even giving up a stringy spit of milky milk.

The brindle cow, she stopped up good.

Jack's momma, she says to him to fetch the brindle cow into town.

Jack, Jack's momma says, fetch that ol' stopped-up cow into town.

She'll fetch a price, Jack's momma says, for her meat if nothing else.

Jack's momma says the brindle cow's hide's done been already tanned by the wind. Her coat, she says, done been wore away. Her horn and hoofs done been hollowed out by the same wind wore the coat clean away.

And she's full-up with all that scrap, Jack's mamma says.

Jack's momma, she tells him to sell the scrap after the slaughter of the ol' brindle cow.

Jack, he says he will.

And the bones, Jack's momma says to Jack, fetch home them inside bones for bread.

Jack, he says he will.

And the tongue, Jack, Jack's momma says, fetch that home too. We can ring it out, ring it dry of water, the water that got leeched from the rust she's been licking from the bob wire.

Jack and the brindle cow, they up and go, gone behind the big ol' cloud wall hanging from the sky and sweeping up cloud of dirt-dust at its feet.

Right away, Jack, he sees nothing but the cloud of dirt all around him.

Jack, he can't even see the brindle cow on the other end of that there rope.

Jack, he nickers. Jack, he says, come, boss, he says.

Jack, he hears the brindle cow say moo. Jack, he can't see her inside the dirt-cloud all around.

This went on for a spell.

Then Jack and the brindle cow come to the forest. Jack, the brindle cow, and the forest are all in the dirt-cloud all around.

The forest weren't made up of no trees. It were a forest of old windmills. Hundreds of windmills. Hundreds. The windmill blades make an aching sound in the gloom when the snaggletooth blades turn in the gritty dirt-wind.

The snaggletooth blades turn over out of sight inside the gritty ground-up dirt-cloud there overhead Jack and the brindle cow mooing in the gloom.

The windmills, they are only milling wind.

The windmills' screw gears, they done been wore away, been stripped clean by the gritty wind.

The windmills can't lift no water. No water to lift.

The windmill in the windmill forest done sucked up all the water out of the ground hereabouts long ago. The windmill forest, it is sinking into the ground, into the hollow place where all the water used to be.

All them windmills, they can't lift no more water. No water to lift. The windmills, they pump sand.

Jack and the brindle cow, they walk through the forest of the crisscrossed windmill towers, the windmill blades making their aching sound overhead.

The brindle cow, she hole-up, stops to take a bite from the wood on one of them crisscrossed windmill towers. The brindle cow, she can't be budged.

That's when a man, he's been there all the time, says to Jack, say, what you got there at the end of that rope?

Jack, he says back to the man that he has a brindle cow all dried-up he taking to slaughter somewhere over there on the other side of the dirt-cloud.

The man, he says I can take her off your hands, says he's got something here way better than a dried-up brindle cow to trade.

Jack, he considers this for a spell.

Jack, he considers all the digging he's been doing, trying to keep his daddy in the ground. Jack, he considers what his momma said about the scrap metal and the hide and the sopping tongue and such.

Jack, he considers the big bones inside the brindle cow and the bone bread his momma wants to make with them.

The man, he says, after a spell, says what's it going to be?

Jack, he says to the man to tell him what's he got.

The man, he takes out a glass vial, a vial stopped up with a rubber stopper. The man, he holds it up right up to Jack's eye so as Jack can see into it.

Jack, he looks and looks.

Jack, he sees inside there an ocean of silver in the vial. An ocean, it has itty-bitty waves breaking and everything. Silver spume and such.

Jack, he is fair amazed.

The man, he says that that there is beads of quicksilver eating each other up. That there is melted metal that don't need no fire to melt. That there is magic beads.

Jack, he can't take his eyes off of them beads of quicksilver swallowing each other up inside the glass vial.

The man, he says this here is the rarest of the rare. Metal made out a water, water made out a metal. You go and spread that there metal-water on any ol' ground and see what grows up.

Jack, he's done thinking.

Jack, he up and takes the glass vial with the beads of quicksilver from the man right there and then.

Jack, he hands over the rope to the man. Somewhere out there on the other end of the rope is the brindle cow.

The brindle cow, she moos in the gloom.

Jack, he hears the man and the brindle cow go off thataway.

Jack, he turns the other way for home. The quicksilver in the glass vial, it gives off its own kind of silver light in the gloom.

The windmill blades over Jack's head, they make that aching sound, turning in the dirt-wind up inside the dirt-cloud.

This went on for a spell.

Jack's momma, she asks Jack what he's got to show for the brindle cow. Jack's momma, she's been waiting for Jack for a spell. Dirt-drifts, have drifted around her skirts where she waited for Jack on the house stoop.

Jack, he showed her there then what he had to show for the brindle cow.

Jack, he showed his momma the glass vial glowing in the gloom, filled up with the itty-bitty ocean of water-metal and metal-water.

Jack's momma, she's angry.

Jack, says Jack's momma, what about all that scrap metal and the leather tanned by the dirt-wind and the waterlogged tongue of that ol' stopped-up brindle cow?

Jack's momma, she says what about the big bones I was going to grind down to bone meal to make our bread?

Jack, he says to his momma that there is quicksilver inside the glass vial, the rarest of the rare. Metal that ain't hard like metal. Water that ain't wet like water.

Jack, he says, there ain't no telling what it can do.

Jack's momma, she don't say nothing, takes the glass vial right out of Jack's hands. The quicksilver inside the glass vial, it's glowing a little in the gloom.

Jack's momma, she considers for a spell.

Then, sudden-like, Jack's momma, she up and unstops the stopper there and just like that pours the water-metal metal-water on the ground.

The quicksilver is quick, quicker than quick, glows in the gloom as it slides through the dirt-air to the ground.

Jack's momma, she says this here is not worth a bucket of warm spit.

The quicksilver, it splashes on the ground. Where it splashes it kicks up little clouds of dusty dust. The way the quicksilver splashes, it makes a wet pattern like a map of the world 'cept the wet parts is the land and the dry parts is the vast ocean tracks I have only heard about in stories.

Jack and Jack's momma, they look down on the ground where the quicksilver makes a map of the world in the dirt.

Both of them stare as the silver-wet of the quicksilver sinks into the dirt-dirt, making a patch of gray mud that, right there and then, begins to dry up on the spot. But it isn't so much drying up as it is drying down. The wet soaking into, seeping into that ground-up ground.

Jack and Jack's momma, they both stand still for a spell. They watch what little wet there was in those quicksilver beads turn into a big ol' dry.

In no time, even the big ol' dry, it's all dried up or, more exact, all dried down.

Jack and Jack's momma, they stand stock still for a spell. Still long enough that the drifts of dirt begin to cover Jack's feet. Still long enough for the drifts of dirt to begin to cover the hem of Jack's momma's dress.

Enough, Jack's momma says after a spell.

Not enough, Jack thinks after another spell of saying nothing.

And both of them fall asleep then and there.

This goes on for a spell.

Then, after a spell, in the dark-dark of the night, Jack, he wakes up to take a leak. Jack, he wakes up and gets up from his pallet of hard-packed dirt. Jack, he goes outside in the yard to make water.

In the yard, Jack, he makes water. The yard, it is so dark, Jack, he can't see the leak he is taking.

Jack, he hears the water he is making hit the ground. The water, it sounds like it sizzles when it hits the ground-up ground, sizzles like it turns to steam the second it strikes the ground.

After Jack takes a leak, after he has made water, Jack he goes back inside to his pallet of hard-packed dirt.

That night is when the thing grows up out of the ground-up ground.

The thing didn't need no sun to grow since it growed up in the nighttime.

That nighttime while Jack and Jack's momma sleep on their pallets of hard-packed dirt, the thing commences to grow.

First, there is this wrenching sound followed by a thumping bunch of big ol' hollow booms followed by a slide-whistling scale with each of them booms is a string breaking on an out-of-tune fiddle followed by the kinks being peened out of an ol' wash-board followed by a mucus-y pneumatic sneezing followed by the crinkling up of a tinfoil ball the size of the moon followed by the lumbering howl of a two-handed whipsaw being doubled up and honed with a horsetail bow to within an inch of its life to play a kind of toothy crosscut lullaby of ripped-up half notes cut in half. And all of this followed by the ears of Jack in the dark-dark, a dark darker than dark on account of the dirt-cloud doubling the dark of the night.

Then, in the dark, there commences the no-mistaking-it sound of water running, water banging in plumbing that hasn't been bled yet, water glugging through too narrow a gauge pipe, water over a rapid, water filled with air bubbles, water fizzing with seltzer. Water plumb out of its mind.

In the dark-dark, Jack had heard it all. Jack, he heard the metal sounds and the water sounds growing together in the dark-dark.

In the morning, when the dark of the dark turns less dark and the dark become more of the regular gloom, Jack, he gets up off his dirt pallet and sees what he can see.

Jack, he sees that it is no longer dark-dark like the night but he also sees it isn't the regular gloom. The thing that growed through the night with sound of metal and sound of water is so big as to cast a shadow on all the shade.

Out of the ground-up ground all around the wind-stripped wood of the wore-out house of Jack and Jack's momma, Jack, he sees these big ol' struts made of metal.

Jack, he sees a grove of these big ol' struts all studded with rivets all trussed up and down with guy wires growing out of the ground-up ground.

The big ol' struts, they're all riveted up and rigged all around with guy wires and rat lines, the big ol' struts also got rungs.

The rungs, they're tack-welded to the big ol' struts.

Jack, he looks up into the depths of the gloom of the dirt cloud. Jack, he looks deep into the cloud.

Jack, he couldn't see no end to the big ol' struts growing up together into the depths of the dirt cloud.

Jack, he grabs hold of one of them tack-welded rungs. Jack, he commences to climb one of them trussed-up struts.

Jack, he has no idea where he's going.

Jack, he has no idea where he's going but he gets going, climbs up them tack-welded rungs, hand over hand, up into the depths of the dirt-cloud.

The climb, it takes a spell.

After a spell, Jack, he looks back down from the rung he is hanging on to, back down through the rigging of the guy wires and rat lines going every which way between the big ol' struts. Jack, he sees nothing down below but the dirt-cloud and nothing up above but more cloud.

Jack, he commences to climb again.

Jack, he climbs up those rungs so long and so far he sleeps in the rigging of the guy wire and the rat lines.

After a spell of more climbing up the rungs and more sleeping in the guy wires and rat lines, Jack comes to the top of the dirt-cloud.

Jack, he pokes his up above the top of the top of the dark ground hugging dirt cloud. And Jack, he sees out over the vast plain of the top of the dirt cloud, a desert of dirt cloud, and floating above that desert are cloud-clouds, all white and lovely-like.

Jack, he pokes his head through the top of the dirt cloud, sees the cloud clouds stretching above the dirt of the dirt clouds, and then and there he ends up on a catwalk.

Jack, he ends up on this here catwalk after all that climbing up the rungs of the big ol' strut.

This here catwalk, it rings around a big ol' cloud, but this big ol' cloud is different from the white and lovely-like clouds floating all around it in the clear clear air above the dirt cloud.

This big ol' cloud, Jack, he sees it's all made out of metal, metal studded all around with rivets and such. The big ol' metal cloud is being held up by the big ol' struts with the guy wires and the rat lines right at the top of the dirt cloud. The big ol' metal cloud, it looks like it is floating there, a big ol' bar of soap floating on top of a bathtub of dirty cloud-water.

Jack, he walks for a spell on the catwalk.

Jack, he walks on the catwalk and on one side, Jack, he sees the white lovely-like clouds hanging in the deep blue sky and on the other side, Jack, he sees the sheet metal of the big ol' metal cloud with its rivets and seams and such.

Walking on the catwalk, Jack, he comes to a hatch cut into the metal of the big ol' metal cloud.

Jack, he climbs through the hatch, he climbs inside, the big ol' metal cloud and inside there, there is this here other catwalk that Jack climbs down onto.

It is dark inside that big ol' metal cloud. It is dark and Jack, he waits a spell until his eyes can see the light that's in the dark.

And in the light inside the dark, Jack, he sees nothing but water. Inside the metal cloud, Jack, sees nothing but water in an ocean of water stretching away to forever and ever.

Inside the metal cloud, Jack, he sees this ocean as far as he can see. This here ocean, it looks like an ocean with ocean waves breaking over each and such right up to the catwalk where Jack, he's standing.

Inside the metal cloud, the breeze in there is freshening. The freshening breeze, it sails over the endless ocean, over the breaking waves and such, and lights on Jack's grimy sweaty face.

Jack, he just lets that breeze light on his face. Jack, his face, it is all grimy and sweaty. And the breeze sailing over the ocean washes all that away.

The breeze, it lights on Jack's face with all its grime and sweat from climbing up into dirt cloud, from living on the ground-up ground for so long.

The freshening breeze, it lights there, it licks the grime and the sweat right off of Jack's face.

This goes on a spell.

And Jack, he commences to cry right then and there. Jack, he's crying on that there catwalk, looking out over that endless ocean he sees in the light of the dark.

Jack, he cries these big ol' tears. These big ol' tears they roll down oncet grimy and sweaty skin of his face. And the breeze lighting there freezes them right then and there.

That's when a woman, she's been there all the time, says to Jack, say, what you got there on your cheek?

APP RO X I M ATE

In the distance, Mason, receding in the distance, trailing the chain, a straight line vectored into a vanishing point on the beam of the horizon.

The blue of the Blue Ridge M o u n t a i n s looks like

At the courthouse, no one could produce a pen.

All maps distort, are distortions, distortional.

HEINRICH SCHLIEMANN, the discoverer of ancient Troy, made the fortune he used to discover ancient Troy selling indigo dye to the Union army.

The high-tension power lines transmitting electricity parallels the parabolic curvature of the Shenandoah River watershed.

Escape velocity can be imagined as

The ~~blue of the~~ Blue Ridge dissipates in the gray rain as if

Before entering the courthouse, Grant stops to lick his thumb to then wipe away a splatter of red clay mud on his right boot only to find the mud to be a fleck of **blood**.

The   panting   steam

engine working a grade in the valley sends up a code of ~~smoke~~, a meditation in clouds…

The last case heard here was a property dispute that remains *unresolved.*

The Blue Ridge Mountains etch a pattern like _____ against the gray sky.

A forgotten observation balloon tethered to a caisson is left to rot in a field of red clover in bloom.

Dixon draws an X in his notebook, erases it, and moves it to the right an inch, in scale, solid soiled in smudges.

The North named battles after the nearest **river** while the South named battles for the nearest **place**, the illusion that they never occupied the same space at the same time.

The *sound wave* a train produces steaming up the Shenandoah Valley warbles as it approaches.

In the distance, the Blue Ridge dissolves in the ~~soaked summer air~~ .

A moth has gotten to the General's gray sleeve, unraveling a **hole**.

My son, a baby then, picks up a slice of an apple left on Traveler's grave by a visiting Son of the Confederacy and attempts to eat it.

Zeno's paradox suggests a bullet c̶a̶n̶n̶o̶t̶ transverse a distance like this sentence can nev

An aide de camp collects the tears of his general in an empty blue bottle he found left in a drawer.

The surveyor for Walmart® stakes the parking lot perimeter with splintered sticks tipped with *red* flags.

Early studies of artillery

contemplated the physics of
projectiles and the force of
gravity working upon its forward velocity like

Grant>Lee

An artists reenacts the saturation of canvas with water in order to create that
cloudy brooding quality, in order that
the fabric not **take** paint.

A CONVENTION OF REANIMATED WILLIAM FAULKNERS

The Parthenogenetic[1][i] Cloned William Faulkner

The Time Traveling William Faulkner[2][ii]

~~The past is never dead, it is not even past.~~

The past is never over. It is not even past.

[1.] It was Antony, "Antler," Pruitt, the blacksmith from the SW corner of The Square, who rushed to Roanoke, dispatching the sledge on the hard-panned forehead of Faulkner Pantokrator as he lay supine on the side porch, spilling out the contents of his thought, a self-reflection of self, now bright-eyed before him, there on the rag rug of braided old dish towels (dish towels once used to dry the saucers and cups, a dogwood pattern, made by the Syracuse China Company of Syracuse New York), naked, yes, but in every way remarkably the same, save for the first thought he was having which was to think of himself as a himself and not as a self thought of by some other thought or thinker of himself.

[2.] There is the rip in time when, during the filming of a documentary at Roanoke, he is filmed watching a distressed copy of a copy of a copy from the Janus Collection of Chris Marker's *Le Jetee*, in a style similar to what he is watching, a series of stills, projected on the white bedsheet, upon which, years before, he was born, so white as to embody the body of absence, beneath a verdant canopy of pine trees where, there, hidden in the somnambulant branches, cicada saw sibilantly through the evening which had been passing at 24 frames per second per second squared but, at that second, stuttered near the speed of light the projector was projecting through the celluloid window of the film, a splice spliced into the quantum physics of the evening sun, the slow and ever slowing rotation of the planet skidding to a stop through the rough and tumble thimble of friction attributed to the heavens…

A **Convention** of Reanimated William **Faulkners** Meets in The Oxford, Mis(s)is(s)ip(p)i, to **Workshop** Their Individual Versions of Playing a Rubber of **Extinct Bridge** and

The Digitally Enriched Holographic Projection[iii][iv] of William Faulkner[3]

> "The past is never past, it's not even past."

[3] He found himself, once again, sitting at his desk at the postal substation on the campus of Ole' Miss examining with a jeweler's loupe, the rotogravure of a stamp that appears to be a commemorative of his own life for in it he is, or a likeness of him is, pictured, smoking a pipe whose smoke is pixilated in an infinitely regressive dot matrix matrix of smoke where each period of ink contains a myriad of information encoded in what seems to be an articulated map more detailed than the thing, him, it represents when, at that instant, a fictional character he was just then imagining, yes, it is one of the Snopeses, pokes his head through the Dutch-door asking to purchase a 2 cent stamp pronto.

The Cryogenically[4] Frozen and Reconstituted William Faulkner[v]

> "The Past ain't over, hell, it ain't even past."[vi]

[4] The final exposure of the low-temperature germanium particle detectors at the Soudan Underground Laboratory yielded two candidate events, including the spontaneous regeneration of the biological entity once known as William Faulkner, with an expected background of 0.9 ± 0.2 events.

This was not statistically significant evidence for a signal. The combined data place the strongest constraints on the WIMP-nucleon spin-independent scattering cross section for a wide range of masses and exclude new parameter space in inelastic dark matter models. The Faulkner anomaly, given, what he called, "a little walking around money," was released outside into the wild, where he caught a GM&O southbound freight disappearing from the oscilloscopes of night.

Museum of the Philatelic Ruins Within The Museum of the Ruins of Their Collective **New** Neo-Nano-Novel©, Recently Completed, While Drinking a Variety of Aged Alcoholic **Spirits**

West leads the Spade Queen against your contract of Seven Hearts. How do you play to win all the tricks?

N
A K 7 6 5 4 3
3 2
A K 2
3

West leads the Spade Queen against your contract of Seven Hearts. How do you play to win all the tricks?

S
–
A K J 9 6 5
5 4 3
A Q J 9

William Faulkner[1] regards the spent flower seedpods of the candlestick magnolia collecting in the gutters of Roanoke:

quilted hand grenade
fused in the flower
entropic

William Faulkner[2] watches a woman ironing during an exquisitely hot afternoon. The steam reads the wrinkles out of the cotton. The wet cursive curls engraved on her sweating neck. She hisses a curse under her breath in time with the contraption's whoosh of erasure.

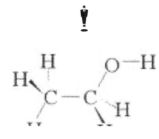

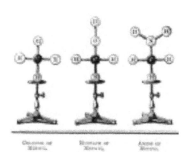

West leads the Spade Queen against your contract of Seven Hearts. How do you play to win all the tricks?

E
2
Q T 8 7
8 7 6
8 7 6 5 4

West leads the Spade Queen against your contract of Seven Hearts. How do you play to win all the tricks?

W
Q J T 9 8
4
Q J T 9
K T 2

William Faulkner, in his role as postmaster, licks a stamp, at that moment purchased by a lady who might very well be a 2nd cousin twice removed. He tastes the particular chemistry of the glue; its atoms grouting the declivity of his tongue, its stickiness sticking, and its bitter taste tacit. The stamp is a window into the letter like an orthodox icon, a hinged door dividing the secular space from the sacred one. Osmotic membrane.

William Faulkner$^{\infty}$ seeks to make the stone stony again. Sometimes, he thinks, the song of the cicada in the pine trees is like the song of the cicada in the pine trees.

[1] The current editors cannot explain the viral free-floating critical comment by a **Michael Martone** found here. The original infection appears to have been initiated in July of 2010 (O.C.) perhaps parasitically **attached** to the acidic molecular structure of **oxygenated cellulose pulp** known as **paper** that ink once adhered to, imported on an antiquated digital carrier circuit from the Benelux region. What we are suggesting is that such commentary is **persistent** and seemingly **immortal**. The text itself is viscous, registering **inelasticity** in the lower range of the spectrum. The editors apologize for their inability to suppress this troubling bubble and for the surplus of **useless information** it contains.

[ii] **It is my ambition to be, as a private individual, abolished and voided from history, leaving it markless, no refuse save the printed books; I wish I had enough sense to see ahead thirty years ago, and like some of the Elizabethans, not signed them. It is my aim, and every effort bent, that the sum and history of my life, which in the same sentence is my obit and epitaph too, shall be them both: He made the books and he died.**

Letter to Malcolm Cowley (11 February 1949, old calendar), quoted in *William Faulkner: A Critical Essay* (1970) by Martin Jarrett-Kerr, p. 46; also published in *Selected Letters of*

William Faulkner (1978 old calendar) by Joseph Blotner, p. 285 (referring to a "page" of a printed book).

[iii] **"The damned thing works!"** - Telegram to one of his backers on 7 September 1927 (O.C.), the day Philo T. Farnsworth transmitted the image of a horizontal line to a receiver in the adjacent room of his San Francisco laboratory. An event horizon of the story's story.

[iv] A Faulkner told a "Jean Stein" in a 1956 (O.C.) interview for the *Paris Review* (?):

> Beginning with *Sartoris*, I discovered that my own little postage stamp of native soil was worth writing about and that I would never live **long** enough to exhaust it, and by sublimating the actual into apocryphal I would have complete liberty to use whatever talent I might have to its absolute top. It opened up a gold mine of other peoples, so I created a cosmos of my own. I can move these people around like God, not only in space but in **time** too

[v] Clocks slay **time**. **Time** is **dead** as long as it is being clicked off by little wheels; only when the clock stops does **time** come to life. A Faulkner from somewhere and some **time**.

ⁿ In 1922 (O.C.) a Faulkner was asked to become scoutmaster of the local Oxfiord Boy Scouts where he specialized in administering the merit badge for **taxidermy**. **Records indicate** he was especially adept at preserving and posing badger, bear, and opossum specimens. Dioramic displays of this **time** attributed to him have been cryogenically treated in the hope that **future** science will be able to reconstitute the suspended Mammalia and **restore them** to the previous state of not not living.

FOUR YEARBOOK SIGNATURES

To a Nice Girl I Met in Freshman English after Mrs.
Wiggs Embarrassed Me in Front of the Whole Class for
Misspelling, Taking My Hand and Talking to It, Saying, "WHERE!" and "WERE!" and "Can You Hear
the Difference, Can You Feel the Difference?"

Later, I felt your breath on my ear, your name breathed into my
brain. You slipped me the note that told were to meet you.

To My Best Friend Sophomore Year Who Got Caught by Mr.
Humphrey Writing Her First Name Over and Over Again Mar-
ried to My Last Name, Practicing Her Made-up Signature When
She Was Supposed to Be Reading the Part of Lady Macbeth

Later, we laughed about being laughed at, happy now everybody
knew we where a we. And later later you said my first name over
and over like it was a poem or something.

To a Girl I Wrote Stuff for in Mrs. Neuhaus's Class
While We Studied Carol King's *Tapestry* and Who Was
Famous for Being the Reserve Cheerleader Who Mis-
spelled the Traditional North Side Cheer, T-E-E-M

Later, the yellow stains of nitric acid from Dvorak's chem lab left
on my fingernails finally grew out, and I thought then that, then,
I would be over you then and, then, I wasn't over you even then.

To a Great Girl Who Cried So Sweatly in Mr. Lewinski's
Senior Seminar When We Read *Tess of the d'Urbervilles* and
Will Go Far in Muncie at Ball State as an Actuarial Scientist

Later, I will find out that this means your life will be taken up by
the calculations of death. You will make tables of numbers. Odd,
I imagine you ask yourself every day since those diminished days
in high school, what were the odds that we would ever meet, that
we met, that we will ever think of meeting ever again?

AMISH IN SPACE

Crewman Yoder, J.: They disappear into the dark outside the ark. It is as if their plain suits absorb what little light there is. I see them as black shadows sliding through space. They blot out the spackle of stars in the background. The toolboxes they carry do flash and sparkle with light from several nearby suns. I can follow the glint whipping along the tether lines to the emptiness at the other ends. There are hundreds catching up light in a web in the dark darkness. They are raising the barn on the starboard nacelle. The framing is finished. I am to help in the making of the coffee. The shadows will be cold and thirsty when they come back inside after working so hard all through the night.

Crewman Yoder, M.: Most of us had never been in a car let alone an airplane when they loaded us on the jet that creates the weightlessness. The cattle were lowing in the corners of the cabin as we climbed. The chickens compressed in their nests. I looked at the children, puddles on the floor, clutching the little paper bags the English had given them to use if they got sick. I could not move as if the thumb of God pinned me there on the matted floor. Until. Until the moment we began to float. Lifted, drifting through the air. The English flying around us held us steady, shouted instructions in all the loud whooshing noise. The chickens were squawking clouds. The cows ballooned, bellowed, shat, and the shit spread lazily in long streaks in all directions. The children made sick, missing the bags that tumbled freely through space. I bounced off the padded walls. The air in my lungs all left. My skin slacked. My hair came undone. I couldn't close my eyes. My arms and legs went their own ways. And then, like that, we all fell back down, collapsed to the floor in piles and heaps. Us and the English and the animals and the shit and the sick like rain and the straw all on the floor, now everything and all of us twice as heavy as before we fell.

Crewman Yoder, Z.: The rockets were larger than the largest silos we had ever seen. They were like silos on top of silos. And they were supported in the cages, the scaffolding of cantilevered gantries that we used to paint the rockets' skin. The bishops argued with the English that the white-and-black design would not do, was not plain. The English said the scheme was best for the pictures they would take. And the bishops told them there would be no pictures anyway. So there I was in a breeches buoy suspended from an I beam up near the top, brushing on the blackest paint you would ever never see on my part of the rocket. The smell of it made me miss the smell of the fermenting grain put-up back at the Goshen silo. The baking wood, the rust on the staves, the barn swallows and the purple martins circling overhead. I was weightless, floating in front of the curving metal plates as black now as the black of space.

Crewman Miller, F.: On the ceiling above our heads, a half a mile away, Crewman Yoder is turning under the five acres of timothy for green manure. In the next field over, his brother, Crewman

Yoder, is drilling beans with the matched Belgian geldings. We are below, in a field of alfalfa, steaming after the first cutting, on our backs between the windrows, looking up into what would have been the clouds caulking the blue Indiana sky on Earth. But now we farm the sky too. Don't tell Father that we are on our backs. We should be in the ditches, weeding tiles. There are polliwogs in the pools, and we are hunting crickets, singing as they warm up in the sun. Through the ground, we can feel the impellers moving the mirror shingles, lengthening the light and casting longer shadows all along the valley of the torus. We mustn't look into the mirrors. There is milkweed nearby caked with cocoons, and we can hear still another Crewman Yoder's bees working around us, looking for a flower that was missed by the sickle.

Crewman Yoder, K.: The old Old Order Amish from Pennsylvania have been asleep for as long as I can remember. The portholes in their vessels allow us to look after them. The beards have all become bushier over time, filling the windows like hairy roots. The women's faces look like dried apple dolls. We keep them in big drawers that slide smoothly into the maple cabinets we built ourselves before the launch. The cabinets are kept in a Quonset hut in the hub. We think of this place as our library. No books but all their family Bibles. Their Bibles and them sleeping, the Old Order Amish with all the chapters of the Ordnung asleep in their sleeping brains, not changing. We meet here, church, for communion in the spring and fall, when we consider what would be worldly or not now that we are out of the world. We cannot decide about the use of Velcro. There are yards of it stowed on board. It is composed of thousands of hooks and eye-like loops. But it may be associated with the military. And yet it will be of great use in all this weightlessness. But it allows a child to fasten shoes without learning from the grandparents how to tie a string. We wonder what the old Old Order Amish will think about this, and all the other things when they wake up at our destination. They will remember all that we will have forgotten over all these hundreds and hundreds of years.

Crewman Yoder, D.: Our farms were near Nappanee. By the time we left, the English had extended the boardwalk completely around us. There were suspended viewing platforms over the fields where I turned the earth with the sulky plow and the sorrel team. Helicopter tours. Spyglasses that magnified our every move. Fort Wayne, South Bend, Indianapolis, had all grown together, leaving only our scattered Amish homesteads, tiny islands, with our woodlots and pastures, the kitchen gardens and hay shocks. The English liked most, I think, the laundry on the line. They posted times when the wash was done and hung, applauding the girls when they had pinned up another garment with the wooden pegs the English women tourists wore in their hair as decoration. We were no longer mere curiosities but now something truly alien, another species. When the English scientists approached the bishop with the mission, we were ready to go. My family, that night, sat on the porch of the old house. We darkened the lamps. We looked up into the big moth-eaten sky leaking light. In the garden, fireflies sparked off of the tasseled corn. Heat lightning flashed in the distance, the white sheets outlining the shadows of the English staring at us in the dark, murmuring on the observation decks and boardwalks, hushing each other not to scare us away, unable to take their eyes off of us.

Crewman Yoder, R.: Only God can create beauty. Our quilts are just that, quilts, practical and plain. We use the Mylar now. There are five or six layers of it in each old suit. The English women at the factory in Delaware gave us lessons on how to piece and sew the goods, patch the bellows joints, and grout the resin-hard shells. But over time the suits wear out, the thermal micrometeoroid garment peppered by the stardust. We delaminate the metallurgical layers. We find solid colors there—black, blue, yellow, brown, a copper red. There is a sheen that borders on the gaudy but that is due to the bias, or lack of one, as the cloth has been extruded instead of woven. An Amish quilt looks plain, since only plain colors are used. No printed fabrics, nothing frivolous or pastel. Not showy. We work together on the topstitching, the quilting itself, but that is after the piecing is picked out by one or another of us. Even though we all sew, we can recognize whose stitch is whose, this needlework or that. It is like handwriting. We know each other's hands. Before the English let us board they asked us strange questions to see how we think, I think. One of the questions was this: "What are the most beautiful things in the world?" We all answered the same. Our families, our children, our gardens, our quilts. Quilting is for the girls mostly, for the future bride to lay up the useful furnishing of her future home. Quilting is for the bride and then for the woman after her family is grown. She will take up stitching again. We use any piece of fabric we can scrounge for this work, which will sometimes transcend gelassenheit, modesty, if we don't pay enough attention. The English explained the journey to us this way. They used a quilt, in shades of black, stretched tight on its frame. Look, they said, space and time is like this quilt, a fabric that can be wrinkled and folded. They took a darning egg and tossed it onto the quilt.

That is the ark, they said. It wobbled and rolled along the contours as if it read the writing embroidered there. The quilt sagged and stretched, recovered in the weight's wake. That is how it all works, the English said. Your ark. Space. Time. Your journey to your new home. As plain, as simple, as beautiful as that.

Crewman Eicher, P.: In this world there is no worldliness. The English sealed us up in this ark and sent us off on our own. Alone. The worldly world we left behind us. It is a kind of heaven, I guess, here in the heavens. Rumspringa. It is my time for me to find me. It is tradition to let us run around. It is tradition to let us break out of tradition. See the world, they say. See the world before I make the choice to settle down, suffer the baptism, marry. I have looked for this world world in the far corners of the ship. The steerage decks and the storage bays and the mechanical rooms and the radar shacks. In the diagnostic labs, I found how to access the electronic games lodged in the sleeping auxiliary processors displayed on the oscilloscope. A silly trifle to direct a moving square back and forth between two sliding lines. Or to point a spinning arrow that shoots out a string of period-sized bullets at odd shaped objects on a collision course. I can do that for real with the toggle boom. I override the automatic defense array and then sweep clean the drifts of micrometeors and astropebbles from the ship's negatively charged hull. When worlds collide. Grains of sand. Charged particles. The elders have a few underpowered jet packs they hide for the kids to find. You will see a pack of them pulsing through the gangways, playing tag in the holds, or hovering over the hangar deck, scaring the herds of sheep there. Or we hang out with the shunned who live in the airlocks, building their geodesic igloos, tending their flower gardens there. The shunned have broken into the battery lockers and the old NiCads to power ancient media devices that project movies on the plain bulkhead. Strangely, the movies are all about the Amish back on Earth back in the day. I want so bad to be bad. But it is hard to imagine what that might be. Tonight, a group of us is going down to the hog houses to make fun of the old men turning the boars out into the open gilts. I'll use contractions in my jeers. Be vain. Look once more at the pictures in the Sears catalogue. Or later still, we'll hang out in the line at the one sub-space telephone booth and wait our turn to make a collect call to Earth. Random numbers. Hello, I'll say, who's there?

Crewman Yoder, V.: As we approach the speed of light, time slows down to a crawl. I am out in the fields of solar panels miles from the main fuselage of the black ark, over there, like a mountain ridge in the middle distance. I have come here to think, climbing up one of the solar windmill towers to be closer to God. I hitched Chick and her foal, in their pressurized blankets, to the tower struts below. She and the buggy she is harnessed to patiently float a few inches above the collectors: the colt tethered overhead kicks up his heels. I can't hear the creak the turbine makes as it turns over slowly, this being the vacuum of space and all. From up here I like to launch these little missiles back toward Earth. Old Ball jars, really, I toss into our wake. I watch them disappear into the distance, their reflected light catching back up with me at 186,000 miles per second as I race away at nearly the speed of light. Each jar contains a little note for the English we have left behind. I am allowed to use the typewriter, but I mainly write in pencil. I imagine the jars bobbing in our signature exhaust, avoiding this or that gravitational field on the way to Earth, falling really, all those light-years back home. I think of the notes as a journal of this journey. Every day here is pretty much the same. The notes reflect it. There is nothing new under the sun. A time to plant. A time to reap. On Earth we worked to stop the flow of time, resist the arrival of the future to our farms. Now, it seems, we have achieved it here in space. We maintain our routines, as we approach the speed of light. The cows milked twice each day. The eggs candled. The wicks in the lanterns trimmed. I remember all the time we fought against time. We started this journey forty-some years ago. On Earth, we were told all those years ago, a billion years will have passed by now. The Sun is ash. All the planets cold. The horizon in the distance swallowing itself. Before it was ever after, the English on Earth invented every frivolous novelty of change, I suppose. They progressed. Modernized. Were always up to date. We must wait for that news to catch up to us. The windmills all pivot, nudged by the vane, to face a passing comet spilling plasma. The blades pick up speed a bit as the photons freshen. As we approach the speed of light and time slows, I find it is harder to remember what has happened. What has happened and to imagine what will. What will happen. I think I will think it is time to head back to the ark. In the buggy, I will urge Chick up to a canter or let her have the rein. Even at a full gallop, the colt prancing, it will take a better part of the day to make it all the way back home.

THE BLUES OF THE LIMBERLOST
BY VLADIMIR NABOKOV

REVIEWED BY MICHAEL MARTONE

Part collection of prose poetry, part entomological treatise, *The Blues of the Limberlost* by Vladimir Nabokov was collected from a series of 3x5 index cards discovered amongst the author's ephemera. The book traces his *Lepidoptera* collecting expositions into the Limberlost swamp of Indiana, the last primordial swamp left undrained in the upper Midwest, which resulted also in the composition of his most notable novel *Lolita*. Included within the synesthetic text are drawings and photographs of the butterflies, to scale reproductions of the wing scales taken from the Karner Blue, an essay on the local delicacy of the region—the butterflied pork chop—a rewriting of Gene Stratton-Porter's *Girl of the Limberlost* from the point of view of a visiting entomologist, a coupon redeemable for a podcast recording of the Luna moth calls of east central Indiana hardwood swamps, and a typographical study of the Cyrillic alphabet based on the genitalia of the male members of the genera *Madeleinea* and *Pseudolucia*.

FOUR HUNDREDTH FORTY-
FOURTH NIGHT, GIVE OR TAKE

She has lost count. She hopes someone is taking notes. All the stories are beginning to run together. This hero with that one. Her catalogues of beauty almost spent. The twists and turns turned and twisted inside out. She sifts through dregs of descriptions to describe nether parts and novel regions. She is coming close to exhausting the metaphors for coming. Yet it is not the close approximation of repetitive renditions that sends him to sleep. There he is. The he of him, across the bed. He is at his peak, peeking at her through the veils of his shuttered, buttered-up bedroom lids, projecting tonight's innovative variation, a critical interpolation, his own story, this nightly news. All these nights and no two nights are alike. Unique. She continues her new new nightly tale. He commands her to present her tail. This night it will be, for both, a feinting action, a pincer move, encircling. He arranges, once again, a permutation of the hundreds of pillows to correspond with the incremental perturbation of her rising action. This, too, this this tonight is something new, is something new, there is always this new something in it, an element, in it, always, that is, there is this variation, this slight surprise. Each night, she narrates through each night's newly conceived physical articulation of his desire, as he places her right arm just so, chocks a knee here, shims and levels. She is inside her story as he is inside her, nearing the end, not the end end of the story but the stopping place for this one night as he nears, at her other end, his end, the mechanical winching of the plot, the appearance of the goddamn Allah *ex machina*. Even now, she narrates this completely new and surprising sequence of imaginary event. He says again and again and again—don't stop, don't, stop don't, stop—behind her in a pitch and with a rhythm that is, yes, unexpected, unanticipated, unprecedented. She digresses, commences the nightly windup, the ululation of dramatic action as he, as he, as he— what is the word, what is the, what is the word—as he… She fills his silence after the after with a sidebar, a foil, a foreshadowing, a plot point that has, just now, occurred to her, a peg to hang her habit on. She continues to tell the telling of this night's new story until its sigh of suspension, continues until it will, it will be continued, and she, she is always restless as he wrests from her, she already spooled and spun almost out even as he begins, as he falls, as he falls asleep and enters again the narrative of his nightly dream, another harem where he has his way with an encyclopedic parade of silent virgins, one after another, and then without distraction, double take or flashback kills her, then her, then her and the very same her again and again again.

THE 20TH CENTURY

WATER LEVEL ROUTE

In the 20th Century, the train named The 20th Century left New York for The Heartland, an all Pullman Consist, plying the mainline rails of the old New York Central known then and now as The Water Level Route.

CONSIST

On August 22nd, 1938 in the 20th Century, the consist of the train named The 20th Century consisted of:

Class J-3a (4-6-4 *Hudson*) steam locomotive: NYC 5450;
Class MP Postal car: NYC 4857;
Class CS Baggage-club car: NYC *VAN TWILLER*;
Class PS Sleeper (17-roomette): *CITY OF CLEVELAND*;
Class PS Sleeper (17-roomette): *CITY OF DAYTON*;
Class PS Sleeper (8-section 1-drawing room 2 compartment): *CENTACORRA*;
Class PS Sleeper (6-section 6-double bedroom): *POPLAR PARK*;
Class PS Sleeper (6-section 6-double bedroom): *POPLAR HIGHLANDS*;

Class PS Sleeper (6-compartment 3-drawing room): *GLEN ANNA*;

Class DA Dining car: NYC 654;

Class DA Dining car: NYC 655;

Class PS Sleeper (6-section 6-double bedroom): *POPLAR GROVE*;

Class PS Sleeper (13-double bedroom): *MACOMB HOUSE*;

Class PS Sleeper (13-double bedroom): *PRINGLE HOUSE*;

Class PS Sleeper (13-double bedroom): *ONONDAGA COUNTY*;

Class PS Sleeper (13-double bedroom): *ASHTABULA COUNTY*;

Class PSO Sleeper-Buffet-Lounge-Observation (1-drawing room 1-single bedroom): *ELKHART VALLEY*.

RED CARPET

In the 20th Century, the train named The 20th Century, train #25, was an All Pullman Limited that departed daily from The Terminal, Milepost 0.0, each night at 5:00P (Railroad Standard Time) from Track 34, Westbound for The Heartland; the passengers boarding the train walked The Red Carpet that was rolled out, 100 yards along the high platform, the crimson pile woven with silver threaded letters, spelling out the train name, The 20th Century, in a streamlined stripes and san serif lettering; and The Conductor tipped his conductor's kepi with one hand while the other hand held the pocket watch he watched as each passenger walked the 100 yards of The Red Carpet toward the doorway to the doorway of The 20th Century to be greeted there by The Conductor and given, by The Porter in a white tunic, a red carnation for the gentlemen and vial of perfume, named after The 20th Century, for the ladies, and then, after all were on board, cleared his throat and announced in a confidant voice the single word "'Board!'"

THE UNIFORM CODE OF SAFETY RULES

SAFE Employees make a SAFE railroad. With SAFE employees, a railroad devoid of any mechanical safety devices CAN and WILL be operated safely.

Fog, rain, sleet, snow, and other adverse weather conditions cannot and will not cause personal injuries, if the individual is a SAFE individual and knows how to function safely under such conditions.

CONDUCTOR

In the 21st Century I am The Conductor on the train named still The 20th Century, and we have our Orders: Westbound, Depart The Terminal (Milepost 0.0), underground, emerging from the tunnel in The Heights and run Wrong Main on the Eastern Shore Line of the Hudson at Harmon (Milepost 32.7) crossing the river where it is not on fire at Albany (Milepost 142.2) with The Passenger Consist and proceed on The Main Line of The Water Level Route, Highballing with All Due Speed and obeying, when necessary, all Slow Orders but with no Meets or Passes, no sidings to be taken or trackage rights utilized or switches to be aligned or moves in reverse, only The Passengers to be transported, deliver safely and on time into The Heartland.

SLOW ORDERS

Westbound Slow Orders for the train named The 20th Century, and we are to proceed with caution, slow running as these rivers of The Water Level Route are still on fire:

The Grand River
The Huron River
The Maumee River
The Sandusky River
The Buffalo River
The Cuyhoga River
The Oswego River
The Mohawk River
The Upper Hudson

OBSERVATION

As The Conductor of the train named The 20th Century, I ride at the tail end, the very last car, in what would have been, had this been the 20th Century train named The 20th Century, The Observation Car, but what is more accurately called The Caboose, also known, in the 20th Century, as a "crummy" or a "way car" or a "hack" or a "bozo wagon" or a "stay safe" or a "monkey wagon" or a "crumb box" or a "bobbler" or an "ape cage" or a "cabin car" or a "shove box" or a "kitchen car" or a "hack flat" or a "gorilla cage" or a "parlor shack" or a "go-cart" or a "shove car" or a "whiff wagon" or a "motel 4" or a "brain box" or a "brain car," "brain" because that is where the brain of the outfit, me, The Conductor, lodges.

CONDUCTOR

On the train named The 20th Century, I am The Conductor, The Brains of the Outfit, and together with The Engineer, The Fireman, The Brakeman, The Flagman, The Pullman Porters, The Passengers, and The Passengers' Pigeons I am Westbound and Highballing at 10 miles per hour, having left The Terminal and heading for The Heartland one thousand miles away.

BLIND

In the 20th Century, when named passenger trains like The 20th Century were pulled, on The Head End, by steam locomotives, hobos desired to "ride the blind," the space between the steam locomotive's tender and the first car that followed in The Consist (usually a baggage car) protected by the unused gangway gasket of the vestibule, protected from the elements and the eyes of The Engineer or The Conductor; there in The Blind of The Limited, a coveted seat, the stowaway right down the line, not stopping, into The Heartland.

OBSERVATION

In the 20th Century, in The Consist of the train named The 20th Century, The Observation Car was an enclosed observation car with the streamlining lightweight design of the carriage walls forming a tapered U shape toward the rear, and there, that observation car did not have, as many other named trains did, a rear-facing glass door that led to an enlarged canopied porch-like open decked viewing platform enclosed by an elaborate railing, installed with a drumhead light that advertised the name of the train or the railway it ran on, all to give the passengers a pleasurable viewing experience of looking into the past, back to where the train had already been and to note, with additional pleasure, the optical illusion of perspective as the parallel rails in the train's wake merged together in the fading distance; I have on this train, named The 20th Century, The Observation Car equipped with such a platform, and I do like to stand on the deck facing rearward as we roll Westbound and Highballing, seeing the throbbing light of the various fires illuminate the dwindling and darkening horizon in our wake, watching the rails of The Water Level

Route weld together at what The Rules of Perspective call The Vanishing Point.

THE UNIFORM CODE OF SAFETY RULES

33. Employees MUST:

(a) Secure raised windows to prevent their falling.

(b) Use every precaution to prevent fires.

(c) Dispose of garbage, bottle, ashes, or other refuse material at designated locations.

(d) Avoid objects, obstructions, holes, and openings, etc., to prevent tripping, slipping, or turning ankle.

(e) Be alert to underfoot conditions that may contribute to slipping.

(f) Employees must stand clear of all tracks when trains are approaching or passing in either direction. They must not stand on one track while trains are passing on another.

(g) Watch and prepare for sudden starting, stopping lurch or jerk when on equipment.

(h) While on running board of an engine, maintain secure handhold.

(i) Place and secure vestibule gates, chains, or bars before uncoupling or separating occupied passenger equipment, baggage, mail, or express cars.

(j) Replace and secure in a position clear of tracks, apparatus used in taking fuel, water, or sand.

WATER LEVEL ROUTE

In every direction, 360 degrees, I observe from my perch in The Observation Car how flat the flatness of The Water Level Route is as it stretches out in all directions (and stretches back through time) around the train named The 20th Century; the flatness only disturbed by drumlins of ruins, knobs and kettles of wrecks of pancaked elevators or collapsed barns or spent and sprung silos or grain bins and bunkers or smoldering water towers or crushed and rusted Quonset huts or splintered storefronts and smoke stacks along crumbling strata of streets that in the 20th Century were named Railroad Avenue running along the mainline of The Water Level Route, and, in the flat distance the flat distance is only disturbed (not by copses of trees or forested wood lots) by copses of leafless turbines (their blades unhinged and splintered) and petrified derrick forests; but The Water Level Route was always more or less level even before this most recent leveling when there were the hundreds of miles of close-rowed corn, postdating the primeval hardwood forest that was cleared to make way for the corn and way before that the endless freight trains of glaciers that ground through the country and then retreated only to return on a kind of schedule, centuries in length, that sanded down (in all directions) the lumpy aggregate that abounded, to sand, created the biased underlayment of the same sameness that would become (all these centuries later) The Water Level Route that I am—and my eyes are—skimming over all these years of going over going and coming through this smooth though burned over and denuded and buffed and buttered landscape, deserted and abandoned, not stopping and always limited, the vanishing horizon all around me in all directions.

EMPLOYEES MUST

(m) Handle freight, baggage, or material in such a manner that pieces will not fall.

NAMES

In the 20th Century, the train named The 20th Century wasn't the only named train as there were many others which included: The Commodore Vanderbilt, The Empire State Express, The Knickerbocker, The Zephyr, The Ak-Sar-Ben, The Whippoorwill, The Steeler, The Blue Bird, The Blue Comet, The Blue Ridge, The Blue Water, The South Wind, The North Star, The Humming Bird, The Diplomat, The Empire Builder, The Hiawatha, The Hoosier, The Pacemaker, The 400, The East Wind, The Twilight Limited, The Cardinal, The Shooting Star, The Land O'Corn, The Meadowlark, The Night Owl, The Clocker, The Zipper, The Phoebe Snow, The Canon Ball, The Noon Flyer, The Planets, The Southern Crescent, The Peoria Rocket, The Curfew, The Silver Comet, The Silver Meteor, The Silver Star, The Auto Train, The Mercury, The Lark, The Midnight Special, and The Broadway Limited that in the 20th Century raced The 20th Century on the paralleling Right-Of-Way of The Pennsylvania through and through The Heartland.

ON THE FLY

In the 20th Century, crack trains like The 20th Century were Limited, not stopping at stations along the way, the slower trains shunted into sidings so that there would be no stopping to stay on schedule; so The 20th Century, a Limited All Pullman train of the 20th Century needed to take on Orders or Mail or even Provisions while on the move, not stopping, wresting the paper from poles extended trackside by station agents as the train sped by or canvas bags retrieved by hooks from scaffolding suspended overhead the way the superscript "th" levitates next to the car body of the "zero" when I type the 20th the "th" a floating package, a bag of mail brought on board to be sorted as the train raced to the next station where the sorted mail would be launched back out, on the fly, to travel on with the momentum of the train's not stopping only to land on some platform inert, inertia overtaken by gravity.

SAND

In the 20th Century, sand, which is a nonrenewable resource over human timescales, became extinct, consumed by use in hydraulic fracturing; the sand, held in a viscous suspension of water and guar, pumped miles underground to prop open the pressurized fissures in shale layers, disappeared underground, which is unfortunate as sand—glass sand, dune sand, quartz silica sand, volcanic sand, aragonite coral sand, garnet sand, olivine sand—is vital for the operation of a train such as this one named The 20th Century, which uses sand to increase fiction between the steel rail and steel wheel, allowing for the initial forward momentum as well as braking, and the lack of the aforementioned sand necessitates the close inspection of the roadbed by me, The Conductor, of The Water Level Route for small piles of relic sand piles on the ties between the rails, left on the tracks by ancient trains in tiny helpings as they sanded the steel wheels on the steel rails of their trains as they headed, ages ago, Westbound, into The Heartland.

EMPLOYEES MUST

(p) Avoid rubbing face, arm, or any part of body with hands while handling creosoted material.

FINGER LAKES

The Finger Lakes are on fire: Cazenovia, Otisco, Skaneateles, Cayuga, Seneca, Keuka, Canandaigua, Honeoye, Canadice, Hemlock, Conesus, as is The Thumb, Oneida; and the lakes of north eastern Indiana are on fire as well: Crooked, George, Bass, Clear, Barton, Fox, Lime, Long, Gage, Linta, Cedar, Story, Cree, White, Grass, Loon, Big Otter, Jimmerson, Snow, Hogback, Black, Golden, Hamilton, James, and Pigeon.

DEADMAN

At The Head End of The 20th Century; more than a mile away from where I, The Conductor, am stationed in The Observation Car, The Engineer, The Fireman, The Brake Man, and The Flagman operate and maintain the many locomotives, the slugs and slave engines, and the head-end power generator cars while being monitored, for efficiency and safety's sake by Dead Man Switches, augmented with a vigilance control that produces every few minutes (and the amount of time that passes is random) an alert sound (a buzz or chime or chirp) that signals The Engineer, The Fireman, The Brakeman, and The Flagman to depress designated buttons on their consoles, and, if they fail to do so, the train will automatically be placed into a full emergency brake application, and The 20th Century will stop; those beeps, buzzes, and bells are transmitted to me here, all the way at the tail end of the train, by means of radio, and broadcast on the squawk box in The Observation Car which is the way I communicate with The Head End, over a mile away forward, and the crew there at their stations, and how orders are exchanged and messages delivered unlike the ways, long ago, The Head End communicated with The Tail End of The 20th Century in the 20th Century, with flags and flares and torpedoes and lanterns and hand signals and bells and air horns and whistles, the whistles that, even now, The Engineer, even now, still uses to warn those who might be waiting up ahead to cross the tracks at the grade crossing, sounding two long whistles and then one short one and then one long one to signal that we are coming through, and I hear that sound even now, drifting along, over a mile away, breaking over The Consist though there is no one at the crossing, not a chance that anyone up ahead needs a warning as The 20th Century Highballs Westbound.

FURTHER OBSERVATION

In addition to the canopied platform, The Observation Car on this train named The 20th Century also has an extended-vision clerestory windowed cupola, projecting from the roof of The Observation Car that allows me to see in all directions, behind the train and off in the great distances on both sides of the train and forward all along The Consist of The 20th Century, over all The Rolling Stock, The Manifest, all the way up to The Head End and The Locomotives there; and, on the roofs of all The Passenger Cars, I can observe the elaborate systems of The Dovecots for The Passengers' Pigeons, which are also called Lofts or Roosts or Coops or Pens or Houses or Pigeonaires, and what with special apparati in The Observation Car's extended vision clerestory cupola, I can manipulate the many hatches and doors and gates and passageways in order to launch The Pigeons on their patrols and recover The Pigeons when they return from their patrols migrating, like a great river or wide lake, folding and flowing along with the long train and its cargo, The Passengers.

EMPLOYEES MUST

(q) Keep desk and other drawers closed when not in use.

(r) Avoid handling electric switches or turning on or off electric lights with wet hands.

MORE NAMES

A building of rooks, a watch of nightingales, a constable of ravens, a quarrel of sparrows, a band of jays, a charm of hummingbirds, a cast of hawks, a tiding of magpies, a bevy of quail, a wisp of snipe, a flock, a flight, a kit of pigeons; all of these different kinds of birds are gone, of course, lost, but their collective names remain—a murder, a congress, a fling, a cast, a gaggle, a covey, a brace, a brood, a squadron, a host, a rafter, a fall, a party, a flush, a colony, and a murmuration—and I think about those collective names as a (I will call them) dictionary of drones, The Passengers' Pigeons, emerge from the doors and hatches and gateways, portals and passageways of the system of dovecots along the whole spine of the Westbound rolling train named The 20th Century—an exhalation, an atmosphere, a saturation, a sublimation, a steep, a fog, a sleep, a dream.

WATER LEVEL ROUTE

The 20th Century proceeds Westbound and Highballing at a walking pace on Standard Gauge, hot-rolled steel rail of 130 pounds per yard weight in staggered 39-foot lengths in stretches that, here and there, were replaced by continuously welded rail halfway through the 20th Century (a ribbon of steel, a river of steel) so that the rhythmic click/clack over the joints disappeared from running of the named trains along The Water Level Route, but there are sections of joined rail even now that create, even at this low speed, an exhilarating anticipation in me of the next stutter over the expansion joint, a syncopated skip in the sliding static as the steel wheel flange slides over the steel rails, rails that are held by the elliptically bolted joint bars, nestled in the web between the head and foot of the asymmetrical I-beamed profile; and there it is, the "thunk" of the leading wheel of right side of the forward truck of The Observation Car, a kind of heartbeat that matches my slowed pulse, as The 20th Century limps and lumbers through an almost imperceptible downgrade toward The Heartland.

HIGHBALL

Before the 20th Century, before the signals, the semaphores and position lights and colored lamps and before radios and telephones and radio telephones that managed all the train traffic on all the rights-of-way with the help of electricity, the trains used hand gestures of its crews armed with bright flags and at night would be lit by the fire of flares or fusees or torpedoes and by hand-powered signals placed gantries spaced along the rights-of-way that allowed dispatchers of trains to raise and lower flags and pennants and often brightly painted wooden balls that when hoisted to the very top of the signal's pole could be observed by the engineer approaching and indicate that all was clear, proceed with all due speed down the line; today, on The 20th Century, we are Highballing and Westbound, the tracks ahead are all clear ahead while in the cluttered gutters of the roadbed of The Water Level Route I see the discarded rotting ties left over from the maintenance-of-way and, in the edges of the ballast, in standing pools of steaming about-to-burst-into-flame water, a pole or two occasionally with a crooked crossbar and snapped wire of the old telegraphy, and also the gantries and posts of the ancient signals and switches, now long gone, and not needed as The 20th Century is the only train that today plies The Water Level Route, Westbound, Highballing at a walking pace to The Heartland.

FURTHER OBSERVATION

In The Observation Car at The Tail End of The 20th Century, I deploy The Aerostat, a lighter than air aircraft that attains its lift by the envelopment of a buoyant gas, a big balloon or blimp, that is attached to The 20th Century by means of a tether, an umbilical that connects to the Westbound and Highballing train and ferries data from The Aerostat to me, here, in The Observation Car, signals from the various Doppler radars housed aloft, where I can view, as the sweeping hand circles the scanning screens, the enhanced images of the surrounding atmospheres and weathers, the disruptions and disturbances of the sky, the furniture of the clouds—the stratus, the cumulus, the stratocumulus, the cirrus, the altostratus, and the cumulonimbus—and the electronic echoes of the backscattered aluminum tinsel chaff storms that still rage and the topography of the skyscrapers of smoke and curtain walls of the unquenchable fires ascending from the ruined and long-smoldering cities along The Water Level Route—Schenectady, Syracuse, Rochester, Buffalo, Erie, Cleveland, Sandusky, Toledo, Waterloo, South Bend; and there in the mix are the braiding tendrils made up of the blips of The Passengers' Pigeons swirling around The Aerostat, which is peeking over the horizons, playing out on its string, another category of cloud, while that flock, that flight, sends me additional burbling data as their ultraviolet filters and infrared sensors and their speed sampling pitot tubes and radiation detectors collectively sniff the up-drafting convections;

the downward looking Pigeons are downward looking, mapping out the nooks and crannies of the pockmarked landscapes and burning watersheds in mottled shadows the Aerostat casts down from above.

EMPLOYEES MUST

(t) Use torpedoes and fusees for signaling only; care must be exercised to avoid injury from explosion or burning material.

ENCYCLOPEDIA

Aboard The 20th Century, stored in The Observation Car is The Encyclopedia from the 20th Century in many Volumes; The Encyclopedia's gilded-edged pages are now deckled, eaten, years ago, by 20th Century insects such as silverfish, book lice, termites, and roaches, and the pages are foxed and, foxing, a brownish stain that looks as if the pages have been singed, scalded, or burned but that does not always affect the actual integrity of the paper pages, only stains the paper in spots and along the edges; its causes are unclear but may include the light from the sun, atmospheric pollution, acidic contamination that was not completely neutralized during the manufacturing of the paper, fungal growth, the effect of oxidation of the copper or iron or zinc in the rag or wood pulp from which the paper was made, or high humidity; the foxed and moth-eaten volumes of The Encyclopedia I have on hand are Volume B; Volume H; Volume M; Volume W; Volume R; Volume V; Volume C; Volume Annual 1962; Volume G; Volume K; Volume S; Volume D; Volume I, J; Volume Annual 1955; Volume A; Volume L; Volume U, V; Volume E; Volume F; Volume INDEX; Volume 1938, Volume N; Volume X, Y, Z; Volume O; Volume Annual 1981; another Volume H; Volume P, Q; Volume

T, Volume Annual 1926; Volume Appendix; Volume Annual 1996; the other Volume B which I leaf through as we make our way along The Water Level Route into The Heartland.

ON THE FLY

In the 20th Century, the train named The 20th Century was propelled by locomotives powered by steam (or, at least The 20th Century employed steam locomotives for a good part of the 20th Century until the steam locomotives were replaced by electric locomotives powered by diesel engines), the steam produced by heating water in a boiler until it turned to steam and then forced the steam into pistons that drove the driving rods that turned the driving wheels, steel wheels on steel rail, and, with a little sand for traction, drove the locomotive and all the cars of the trailing consist toward the destination, toward the end of the line; because the locomotive ran on steam and because the steam needed water to be made into steam and because The 20th Century was a Limited, a crack train that would not stop until it reached its destination at the end of the line, the steam locomotive that powered The 20th Century had to pick up water "on the fly," which meant the steam locomotive's tender, where the water used for making steam was stored, lowered a scoop that opened below the car and scooped up the water which was stored in mile-long troughs between the tracks (a kind of channeled river, a placid finger lake), scooped up for the locomotive, the locomotive never stopping, and stored in the tender to be used in the future to make more steam to propel the engine that conveyed the train along The Water Level Route through the 20th Century; and even now, centuries later, I can see the ruins (the crumbling concrete troughs, the rusting metal pans) filled with stagnant water smooth and still but on the verge of catching fire there between the tracks going on for a mile or more as they slip out behind the platform of The Observation Car, a kind of matte green carpet wedged between the tracks as they vanish in the distant past.

HOMEWARD BOUND

There are no hobos now who walk The Right-Of-Way of The Water Level Route, but back in the 20th Century they did, the Hobos, also known as "bindle stiffs" or "bums" or "tramps" or "vagabonds" or "drifters," and one of The Conductor's jobs would be to observe, from his perch in The Caboose, the unlawful un-ticketed transit on the train by The Hobo who would ride in the boxcars or the flatcars or the gondolas or the hoppers or the auto racks or the tank cars or the well cars with a single or double stack of containers or no containers at all or the cattle cars or the reefers where in the days before mechanical refrigeration, when blocks of ice were stored in bunkers at either end of the car, the hobos would hide in iceless empty bunkers to go unobserved by The Conductor and sometimes become trapped inside the ice-less bunker on the ends of reefers, the trapdoor locking from the outside, only to die there without water or starve without get-ting where they were going, and that, I think, is where the name "Hobo" comes from, "Home" and "Bound," an abbreviation, an abbreviation of "Homeward Bound" that goes back to the 19th Century and the soldiers of both sides in The Civil War, walking home after being mustered out, walking through all the Private Property by using the Rights-Of-Way of the railroads and some-times, illegally and unobserved, the railcars of the railroads to take them home, wherever that may be, but what always was to them the heartiest of The Heartland.

THE UNIFORM CODE OF SAFETY RULES

A SAFE individual CAN work safely in the dark as well as in the light, if patience, care, and caution are exercised.

DEADMAN

I hear, from The Head End, over a mile away, the diminished chord bursts of The 20th Century's warning whistle (two long, one short, one long) as The Locomotive approaches yet another grade crossing signaled by the sign (a black painted "W" on circle of white) planted yards before in anticipation of the intersection and sonic punctuation The Water level Route's Right-Of-Way has right-of-way to cross the crossing, and then another sounding (two long, one short, one long) as the train continues, and over the squawk box come the warning sounds of the Deadman switch from The Head End cab where The Engineer, The Fireman, The Brakeman, and The Flagman respond to the prompt, indicating by depressing a button that they are still conscious, able to respond to the warnings, but I know that is not true, that there is no Engineer or Fireman or Brakeman or Flagman riding The Head End of The 20th Century as all those designations are obsolete, all have been automated long ago, the various tasks and operations wired into the cybernetic neural net of the train, the droning Passengers' Pigeons feeding crumbs of telemetric data from their sampling clouds, murmurations swarming around The Consist, signaling the binary switch that switches the binary whistle, minor keyed and far way, wave after wave (two long, one short, one short) from The Head End drifting all the way back to me in The Tail End, pretending and tending The Passengers, deep asleep, on this Limited, All Pullman Express, Highballing into The Heartland.

MURMURATION

"The air was literally filled with pigeons; the light of noonday was obscured as by an eclipse; the dung fell in spots, not unlike melting flakes of snow, and the continued buzz of wings had a tendency to lull my senses to repose..." Audubon wrote in 1813, and 100 years later, the dawn of the 20th Century, the last passenger, the endling of the species, died in Cincinnati, a ruined city to the south, where the Ohio River still smolders, I understand, as we now ply further north along the rails, Westbound, of The Water Level Route, and the train's flock of Pigeons, not as vast or numerous as the flocks of old, I suppose, but impressive nonetheless, flow like an undulating pointillist river around and over the silver sides and tops of the shining corrugated streamlined cars that make up The Consist of The 20th Century, so thick in number and synchronized in their aerobatic maneuverings as to be consolidated into one endless skein of organic tissue that folds and unfolds upon itself, an endless printed paragraph with ragged margins left and right, kerned and turning, fine print scrolling page after page, the sound they are making in concert easily drowning out the occasional click/clack of the steel wheel on steel rail below my feet on the criss/cross tread of the aluminum floor plate reverberating in a shudder and thunk through the train, not unlike the ripping of rag paper, an endless zipping tear as they bank and turn and stall and rise in schoolish unison.

PULLMAN

The Consist of The 20th Century is mainly made up of Sleepers as this is an all Pullman train of passenger cars configured into compartments of double berths and dormitories of double or triple bunks that run the whole length of the car or stair-stepped roomettes; there is no need for (and there are none in The Consist) coaches nor day cars nor drawing rooms nor lounge cars nor parlors nor diners as there were on The 20ᵗʰ Century in the 20ᵗʰ Century, neither a barber nor a stenographer nor a manicurist nor a governess for the children as there are no children as passengers now, and The Passengers who are passengers on The 20ᵗʰ Century, an all Pullman Limited, are asleep in their berths, their compartments, their rooms and roomettes, their bunks, and their beds; the output of their telemetry making a sonorous sawing, the tractor fed chart folding into trays I examine and cancel, here and there, punched with my antique ticket punch through the brooding collection of dot-printed matrices of dot, dot, dot, dot.

HEARTLAND

At night as The 20ᵗʰ Century Highballs Westbound, I like to stand in a vestibule between passenger cars, open the top half of the Dutch door letting the air enter as it moves by, in from out in The Middle of Nowhere on The Water Level Route, heading for The Heartland, and the accordion gasket that encloses the gangway between the cars breathes in and out as the train drifts along the rolling ballast of the underlying roadbed accompanied by the creaks and dings and pings of metal sliding on metal, a chain chiming somewhere; I see the night sky through the cloud of Pigeons pacing the train and there beyond the criss/cross cloudy streaks of glowing fossilized contrails that cut through the other clouds ({the cirrus and the stratus and the cumulous} illuminated in the night by those erratic sparks and flashes, a lightning telegraphy) like luminescent ribs of a ship or cathedral nave, the hundreds of contrails that never dissipate, but permeate, permanently boring holes through the sky, tracks and traces of inexhaustible and inarticulate sentences.

THE UNIFORM CODE OF SAFETY RULLES

Safety is of the first importance in the discharge of duty; obedience to the rules is essential to safety and is required; in case of doubt or uncertainty, the safe course must be taken; to enter or remain in the service is an assurance of willingness to obey the rules; the service demands the faithful, intelligent, and courteous discharge of duty; to obtain promotion, ability must be shown for greater responsibility; suggestions from employees intended to promote safety, economy, or improve service, are solicited and will receive consideration.

PUNCTUATION

".," a period; ",," a comma; "?," a question mark; "!," an exclamation mark; "'," an apostrophe; """," a quotation mark; "...," an ellipsis; "-," a hyphen; "-," an en dash; "—," an em dash, ":," a colon; ";," a semicolon; the cars of The Consist are coupled between the cars by couplers, connecting each unit of the train into a train, like ligatures between letters in cursive writing or the ones in type printing—fi, fj, fl, ff, ffl, fa, fe, fo, fr, fs, ft, fb, fh, fu, fy—that look like, now that I print them, like the ties between the rails (known also as "sleepers") that blur together below your feet as you step from one car to the other along the jointed diamond tread gangways over the automatic couplers that hold the train together and make the cars of The Consist; the Janney "Knuckle Coupler" (also known as the MCB/ARA/AAR/APTA Type E, Type F, Type H), I think, looks like, when I look at it from above, the ties oscillations below it, a semicolon of sorts, the period swallowed by the comma, the sudden stop and the long pull of the pause.

WATER LEVEL ROUTE

At night, the rivers that are on fire along with their tributaries, the creeks and brooks and rivulets and springs and streams and kills, all on fire, look like red molten carpets rolled out for The 20th Century, and the night sky I observe from The Observation Car is sparking, showering clouds of meteors that look like flocks of Passengers' Pigeons who in the shadows of the extinguished meteors shadow the meteors' vectors and stalls, their interceptions and evasions; there is no other light but this grounded combustion, this weary incandescence of dying stardust, and the pulsing afterthoughts emanating from the green screens that surround me, refreshing, sweep after sweep, signaling no contact, no bogie, no hostiles, no nothing out there out there.

BLIND

Even in the 20th Century, few people understood the lyric found in Blues songs saying, "I'm gonna leave this town, gonna ride the blind," the sheltered spot between the locomotive's tender and the baggage car of a crack limited, a fast express, like The 20th Century that plied the rails of The Water Level Route from The Terminal to The Heartland and, because it was so fast, scooped up water the steam locomotive needed "on the fly," spring, summer, fall, and winter, and, because it was scooping up water "on the fly," not stopping, the scoop slicing through the water in the track pan, throwing a wake of excess water back toward the blind, super cooled by the winter's winter temperature, the velocity of the spill, and the chilled exposed metal of the streamlined baggage car the splash froze instantly and encased any hobo in the blind in an icy ice sculpture of ice, flash frozen, only to be discovered at The End of the Line deep in The Heartland icily encapsulated on the fly in ice coating the grooves and flutes and baffles of the silver streamlined baggage car of the blind; I think of that as I walk the passageways of the all Pullman Consist, the Passengers all in their berths and bunks, their drowsy robotic Porters monitoring their suspended stasis, the monitors sighing and snoring, electrically dreaming as The Passengers sleep, and in the middle of the night on the platform of The Observation Car, I look back into the past of where the train has been and into the constellations of all the fires burning, singing to myself, the click/clack keeping syncopated time, that I'm leaving, I am riding the blind, waking from what I thought it was to be sleeping only to wake up in The Heartland in The Middle of Nowhere at The End of the Line.

FINAL OBSERVATION

In The Observation Car, I can scan with a bank of scanners the whole spectrum of frequencies, skipping from one modulation to the next, searching the oceans of air for anything (a voice, some music, a baseball game, other named trains plying other routes—The Mainline of Mid America, The Nickel Plate Road, The Route of the Rockets, The Broadway, The Way of the Zephyrs—or even, in the static, the nicknames of railroad reporting marks—The Cheap and Nothing Wasted, The Backward and Obsolete, The Erie Lackatraffic, The Yellow Dog, The Grand Junk, Nights and Weekends, Take Pity and Walk, The Onion Pacific, The Moron, Lousy and Nogood, The I Can't Go, Bashed and Maimed, The Shake, Rattle and Roll) the scanner skipping through the channels

- 07 160.215 Chicago West Pullman & Southern - Yard
- 08 160.230 CSX - Road - Former B&O/C&O
- 10 160.260 CN/EJ&E - Yard
- 11 160.275 CSX - Ready Track
- 12 160.290 CSX - Dispatcher-RB (Calumet City)
- 13 160.305 Terminal Operations
- 13 160.305 Iowa Interstate - Yard
- 14 160.320 CSX - Dispatcher (Calumet City)/SA (Monon)
- 15 160.335 BNSF - Engine House - Cicero
- 16 160.350 CN - Road - Matteson Subdivision
- 18 160.380 Belt Railway - West Yard
- 19 160.395 CSX - Yard - Barr-Westbound
- 20 160.410 UP - Road - Villa Grove Subdivision
- 22 160.440 Metra - Road - Southwest Subdistrict
- 25 160.485 Indiana Harbor Belt - Road - Dispatcher
- 25 160.485 UP - Road - Milwaukee Subdivision
- 26 160.500 Belt Railway - Road - Dispatcher-South
- 28 160.530 CN - Dispatcher - South Bend Subdivision
- 31 160.575 UP - Yard - Global One/Proviso Tower
- 31 160.575 Wisconsin & Southern - Road
- 32 160.590 CN - Road - Subdivision/South Bend
- 35 160.635 Chicago Rail Link - Yard/Transfer
- 35 160.635 CSX - Dispatcher-AW (Grand Rapids)
- 36 160.650 BNSF - Road - Chillicothe Subdivision
- 39 160.695 Belt Railway - Road - Dispatcher-North
- 42 160.740 Amtrak - Yard
- 43 160.755 CN - Road - Freeport Subdivision
- 44 160.770 CP Rail - Road - C&M/Fox Lake Subdivision
- 46 160.800 NS - Road - Chicago Line (former Conrail)
- 49 160.845 CN - Yard - Gateway Intermodal

- 52 160.890 UP - Road - Geneva Subdivision/Rockwell
- 54 160.920 CN - Road - Joliet Subdivision
- 57 160.965 Belt Railway - Hump Yardmaster
- 58 160.980 Indiana Harbor Belt - Road - Dispatcher
- 59 160.995 BNSF - Yard - Corwith
- 60 161.010 NICTD - Road/Mobile
- 61 161.025 Metra - Road - Electric District
- 62 161.040 UP - Road - Kenosha/Harvard Subdivision
- 64 161.070 Norfolk Southern - Yard - Ashland/Colehour
- 65 161.085 CP Rail - Road - Davenport Subdivision
- 66 161.100 BNSF - Road - Chicago Subdivision
- 69 161.145 Union Pacific - Yard - Dolton
- 70 161.160 BNSF - Yard - Cicero/Road - Aurora
- 71 161.175 Union Pacific - Yard - Proviso
- 72 161.190 CN - Road - Chicago Subdivision
- 77 161.265 Amtrak - Car Department
- 78 161.280 Union Pacific - Road - Joliet Subdivision
- 79 161.295 CN - Road - Waukesha Subdivision
- 80 161.310 CSX - Yard - Barr-Eastbound
- 82 161.340 Metra - Road - Rock Island District
- 83 161.355 NICTD - Road/Repeater
- 84 161.370 CSX - Road - Monon Subdivision
- 84 161.370 CSX - Yard - 59th St. Intermodal
- 85 161.385 BNSF - Road - Mendota Subdivision
- 88 161.430 CP Rail - Yard - Bensenville
- 89 161.445 Belt Railway - East Yard
- 91 161.475 CN - Road - Leithton Subdivision
- 91 161.475 Manufacturers Junction - Yard
- 92 161.490 Norfolk Southern - Road - Chicago District
- 93 161.505 Amtrak - Road - Michigan Line

- 94 161.520 CP Rail - Road - Elgin Subdivision
- 95 161.535 IHB - Yardmaster-Gibson West End
- 97 161.565 IHB - Hump Yardmaster-Blue Island

that then returns to the top of the list and scans again searching for something, anything, only to land on an articulate hush— only two long nothings of silence, one short empty of absence, and one long nothing of nothing.

TIME

We have arrived On Time; The 20th Century terminates at The Union Station in The Heartland where, in the 19th Century, the railroads met to establish Railroad Standard Time robbing the sun of its sole power to set time so that the schedules of the limiteds and expresses and locals and milk runs and flag stops and commutes and shuttles and switches and interchanges and transfers and through cars and extras and specials and mixed consists and shunts and meets and dedicated fast freights and holiday charters and tourist run-bys and work trains and business specials and whistle stops and reverse moves and RPOs and fast mails and hazardous materials and cattle cars and reefers and empties and deadhead moves would depart and arrive on time; and on time we cut the Pullman Consist from The 20th Century and set the cut on a siding in the yard of tracks beneath the Union Station and run The Locomotives back around to couple with the Observation Car and then proceed to the wye and wye around so that the depleted Consist now is heading Eastbound and ready to Highball while the Pigeons reconnoiter the canyons and the cliff faces and send back the news that the river here is still a river running the wrong way from a lake that seems to be a lake, and I set the timers that will incubate The Passengers, nudge them to waking, start the clocks again for all of them, who thought, when they went to sleep, they would be transported, transported to another place and thought they would wake up on Mars or the Moon or a moon of Saturn or another Earth or a station in space or in some other solar system or some other dimension but instead will wake up in The Middle of Nowhere in The Heart of Country where the days and days have piled up and where endless nights are stored, a city of big sleeps, the nation's freight handler after all, with plenty of time to think about time on their hands.

DEADHEAD

After delivering The 20th Century, The Conductor will Deadhead, Eastbound, to The Terminal (Milepost 0.0). Those are my Orders. I depart, deadheading, back down The Water Level Route, following the trail of sand and the beacons of fires. The Water Level Route—without the shifting speeds and gravities of mountains and valleys, tunnels and bridges—advertised that the passengers in the all Pullman consist could sleep. The Conductor can never sleep as he is The Brains of the Outfit. And, even now as I Deadhead I find it hard to sleep. I find myself counting things. Not sheep. There are no sheep. I count the countless stars that are still falling. I make lists of lists. I break apart The Consists of trains and assemble them in the classification yards. I listen for the occasional click/clack of expansion joints that disrupts the continuously 130-pound welded rail. Count the sleepers asleep between the rails. Say the names of places. Find the places for the names. Retrieve my orders on the fly. Fill in the blank spaces of the forms. Stay SAFE. Do the paperwork. Punch the tickets. Connect the dots on the maps. Erase the spaces. Train myself to become lost. To lose.

KODAK: THE FILM

REVIEWED BY MICHAEL MARTONE

A week before the iconic film and camera company received the dire warning from Wall Street, threatening the delisting of its shares from the New York Stock Exchange, *Kodak: The Film* opened a limited run to a disappointing box office in select theaters in Los Angeles and Rochester, New York. The film, *Kodak: The Film*, was filmed on what is thought to be the last remaining film stock of Kodak's VISION3 200T Color Negative Film 5213/7213, a formulation the company had hoped would compete with the evolving and less expensive tape and digital recording formats. Found stored in what was once the RKO Radio Pictures Studio building in Culver City later purchased by Desilu Productions and now an independent postproduction facility, the Kodak film of *Kodak: The Film* is iridescent and shockingly vivid in the visual and sonic information it conveys.

Kodak: The Film stars no one really but the material means of production of photographic reproduction—cameras, chemicals, emulsifiers, negatives, filters, film—exposed and not. Narrated by the comedian and educator Bill Cosby who was at one time the company's commercial spokesman, *Kodak: The Film* might be thought of as a documentary docudrama hybrid. It is a 3-D, super-color-saturated version of *March of the Penguins* spiced with the 16mm coarsely grained b&w capitalist-socialist realistic propagandistic shorts made during the Cold War by the AFL-CIO called *Industry on Parade.*

Though these primogenitors suggest movement, what is most striking about *Kodak: The Film* is that it is a movie that does not move, shot, as it is, in a series of stills. The static motion technique of *Kodak: The Film* harkens back to the haunting 1962 film *La Jetée* by Chris Marker who acted, at 92, as a consultant to *Kodak: The Film*'s director Martin Scorsese. The technique teaches the viewer, as the slide show slides by, the filmstrip nature of the film as the film is stripped of its essential illusion of movement. We are asked to appreciate the apparent invisible vibrant and constant nature of light itself, both wave and particle.

Kodak: The Film is itself haunting as it haunts itself, opening as it does with a photomontage of superimposed "found" images salvaged from dumpsters near photo processing labs where snapshots discarded by their owners were discarded. Thousands of pictures of random people posing (one after the other), waving, dissolving into pictures of people in costume—for Halloween, the prom, weddings, first communions—fading into one-hundred years of birthdays—the cakes on the tables, the air made madly solid by the spent candle smoke caught drifting, illuminated by Instamatic flash cubes that are themselves pictured flashing and turning and revealing, in the red afterglow of the flash, the picture after picture of people taking pictures of people taking pictures, the floating pinpoints of light coming to light on the contracted irises of red-eyed starry-eyed startled pets bleeding into the overexposed nebula of nebulous social gatherings, graduations, gardens, grandstands, gratuitous sexual organs.

Kodak: The Film is a paean to point-of-view, to point-and-shoot as the camera pans and pulls, tracks and racks. One is submerged in this new sublime subliminal atmosphere of aperture and f-stop. The light here is a liquid ceaselessly flowing, arranging itself in pixilated pixel patterns that sort themselves into image after image of images of images of actual water of light falling over the High Falls of the Genesee River in headwaters of the river of film, Rochester, NY.

Finally, there is finally no finality to *Kodak: The Film*. It is all collage and cutting. One jumps over the chasm of invisible darkness between the frames, the stutter steps over the stepping-stones, the endless loops, the speeds of stillness going nowhere fast. *Kodak: The Film* is the filmiest film school film filmed. Another section of the film highlights film leaders. It becomes a kind of film within a film film. A number of film leaders, their numbers counting down, lead to a film of numbers counting down. There is a poignant collection of hand-scratched changeover cue marks that promise reels of film that never arrive. The somber *Kodak: The Film* is both record and method of the annihilation of space and time before our eyes. It ends not as a consequence of consequence, nor through the machinations of plot or narrative of cause and effect or character drive or growth or change. *Kodak: The Film* ends in entropy; its final montage sequence pitted against our perceived notion of sequential time.

The movie's whole and wholly on-message message has been this stunning relentless resistance. No beginning. No middle. No end.

The final sequence consumes itself, a rapid-fire firing of the artifact of plastic time catching fire. Pictured are frames after frames of frames spontaneously combusting, melting, dissolving literally, evaporating, jammed and jellied, reduced and rendered, boiled and fried, warped and scorched, effaced, vaporized before your eyes. The sprocket holes gape open like the scream in *The Scream*. This goes on for hours. I mean for hours literally, in homage to Andy Warhol's 1964 film *Empire*, the camera does not look away from this serial sizzling stasis. You are steeped in the banality of boredom, of the repeating images of images of time-lapsed explosion, implosion, of the deep breathing and frustrated sighing of Bill Cosby on the frayed and fraying soundtrack. But you do not want to look away because (spoiler alert!) the next frozen image of decay might actually be the actual animation of *Kodak: The Film*'s self-destruction as all of the prints (and now there are so few left to see) are treated to ignite of their own volition, sooner or later, and disappear completely into volatile vapors and very little ash.

KEY

I work as a substitute letter carrier for the Postal Service.

Let me tell you a secret: There is only one key. I know this because when you get your uniforms and your equipment down at Brateman Brothers on Main—the same place the police and firefighters get theirs—part of the outfit is this one key. There is only one key, and they make a big deal over it. They tell you not to lose it, don't make any copies of it. This key, it's the only one you'll ever need.

The key opens everything. It opens the doors on the red and blue corner mail drops and the green-painted relay boxes. It opens the drawers and slots and cubbies of all the PO boxes. It's the passkey to all the doors, cash drawers and the cash boxes, the cabinets of stamps and forms, and the locks on all the mailbags. Those big long banks of mailboxes in the lobbies of apartment houses open up, all at once, with one twist of this one key. The trucks and jeeps all start with it. The gas pumps in the parking lots unlock with it. Think about it. You can't have a different key for every different building you need to deliver to, every collection box you need to empty. The letter carrier would be a key carrier, thousands of different keys on one big ring. No, there is just one passkey for everything, and everybody—every man or woman down at the PO—has one.

Most of us keep it on a long chain. You don't want to lose it. They make a big deal of that. At the office, it's our own little secret. And when you leave the job you have to turn it in, your key. There are hundreds of them in there, all the same. Any one of them will unlock the case where they are kept. The key fits the lock on that case's door too.

I still walk my route. I park my truck on the end of the street and walk door-to-door. The mailboxes are beside the front doors of the houses, not on poles by the curb. The neighborhoods I work are quiet. Everybody's working or at school.

One day, on a lark, I tried the front door lock with the key, and it worked! I tried the next house and the next. The key fit in all the locks. Finally, I went through one of the doors. No one was home. The key fit in all the locks in all the doors inside the house. It even fit the clock on the mantle. I wound it and set the pendulum moving again. I unlocked the jewelry box I found in a locked closet in the bedroom and unlocked a locket I found inside. I unlocked the lockbox I found under the bed and found inside keys for safety deposit boxes at a branch bank also on my route.

I tell you I was stunned. I sat at the kitchen table, holding the key, looking around for something else to unlock. I had the rest of the mail to deliver. I was tapping the key on the top of the table. The teeth of the key slid into the pattern of the Formica table top, a perfect fit. I slid it out and tried the side of the salt shaker. It fit. The salt spilled out of the little open door. I held the key, regarding its teeth, the grooves and channels. I thought I would try something completely different. I tried the palm of my hand. The key fit my hand perfectly. I opened up the top layer of skin to see

another door made of muscle. The key fit there too. I closed up
my hand and locked it. I centered the key on my forehead and it
slid in. It was painless. I turned the key slowly. The lid of my skull
sprung open—I had taken off the pith helmet. I dropped the key
inside and pushed the lid closed without thinking. It made a solid
snapping sound in my ears. Right then, I made a mental note to
myself: Get another copy of the key.

THE DEATH OF DEREK JETER

Derek Jeter and the Maintenance of Light

There is no clock in baseball. Once a game begins there is a chance, no matter how remote, that the game could go on forever. There's not a clock, not like football or basketball, but there is a clock, a real one, in every stadium, part of the scoreboard, running and running. In Yankee Stadium, it is now a digital clock out in left center field made up of individual lights that arrange themselves into the numbers, the hour and the minutes, two stories tall. During a game, I catch myself stealing glances over my shoulder out beyond the graveyard of dead center. Now and then, I will actually see the lights pulse and blink, change from one minute to the next. Sometimes, I can actually feel time at my back. Feel the seconds accumulate and build approaching that silent shift of 19 to 20, the squared-off center line of the nine disappearing or flipping down to connect with the right-angled foot of the zero. I am shouting out the number of outs to the outfield. Two away, say, signaling with my fingers how things stand. And the time changes just like that. The clock goes on and on in its way. Tick, tick. A moment closer to forever. When I was a kid my whole league took buses to Comiskey where the scoreboard spelled out that the Sox welcomed the teams of Kalamazoo and we watched the fireworks explode above the old-fashioned Elgin clock with hands and hash marks when the home team hit a home run. I remember thinking the clock got stuck as those games wore on. I watched the Yankee box scores get posted by hand, somebody fitting the goose egg into the opening on the green wall. That would be the best seat in the house, up there inside the clock, looking down on the action below, the grinding of the gears in your ears, the hands of the clock casting shadows on the field in front of you, the sun casting its own shadows as time moved. Now in the new Chicago Park the old clock is gone but they have left a hole where it used to be, a big oval frame with another advertisement for bread or beer. Back in Yankee stadium a light burns out in the nest of bulbs that make up the numbers. Mr. Steinbrenner doesn't like to see his clock all snaggly, the numbers looking like numbers they're not. The grounds crew rappels down the face of the green wall, their ropes rigged up to the gingerbread of the famous façade. I like doing it, a big pinstriped pendulum swinging back and forth, a whole crew winching me with block and tackles. I have the new bulb in my pocket. The lights are all blazing so we all can see which one is dead. That close, I am blind, but somewhere deep inside it all is the tiny spot of blackness. I aim for it. "I see it," I shout to the ground. I see it. I lean into the harness and wait for the weight of the whole contraption to come around. It is like following a fly ball into a mitt, but this time I am the fly ball and I am flying, barreling along, bearing down. Suddenly, I swing back toward that wall of light, the light becoming brighter.

Derek Jeter and the Domino Theatre of Eternal Stories

I am down on my knees. The precise space between the dominoes is crucial. You want the falling tile, in its falling, to trigger the next tile to fall. Too close, they can wedge together and, stacked up, stall, stopping the clicking chain reaction. It steadies my nerves. It passes the time. I am working on one long marching line, now, along the wall of windows in my loft where, at the far wall, the column topples up an incline and tumbles off a sudden cliff, sparking as it lands the spontaneous collapse of a 400-by-400 brick field in imploding plastic tsunami, revealing, as it falls, a pointillist portrait—I use both black and white tiles— of Bucky Dent in away grays before the inertia of the spilling pixels breaks apart into several pinstriped tendrils vining around the dining table legs. For awhile there, that hysterical crowd maneuver, the Wave, took off in baseball stadiums, the fans leaping up and plopping down in order in spite of the fact it was a football thing like the stadium card squads who flip through their routines in measured time at halftime. But on the field, I have the best seat in the house when a Wave starts up. I watch that abstract energy flow through the stands and bleachers and sometimes in opposite direction on the upper decks, time and time again until both breakers crash and subside in the pool of people behind the right field foul pole like surf crashing into the piles of a fishing pier. When I finish, the floor and counters, the furniture and the appliances will be completely scaled by these little tombstones of potential energy on the edge. I keep the windows closed. Last November, a sparrow flew into the Frisian Expo Center a few days before Domino Day, and the tiny bird's landing on one random tile in the middle of the four million in place took out 23,000 before the reaction could be stopped. I was there—it's the off-season—a mere field hand tweaking a side shooting spiral jetty to bloom into a herringbone tweed rank-and-file scallop as the main fuse zippers by when the bird fluttered in, skimming at domino-level toward me. I tried to net him in my hat, this hot grounder. Others in the vast arena reasoned in several languages with the bird as it jinked and dived, gave directions, pointed the way back outside. We all knew fate had already been written into the sprawling arrangement at our feet, but who could have guessed this little guest of chaos would settle on that double blank. Finally they shot the thing, and it's stuffed now and displayed in some museum in Rotterdam, but that was after I tiptoed in pursuit, stepping between the island chains and archipelagos of thousands and thousands of dominoes ready to fall. It was as if I were turning two, my eye on this ball of feathers, that little ballet on second I do in my sleep, reversing the direction of flowing momentum, that moment airborne, suspended at rest and wrenching gravity back on itself, wresting it up by its roots. At home, all it takes is a little flick of my finger and that insignificant gesture endlessly carpets, with the spilling bones, the whole vast flat flat.

Derek Jeter and the News that Stays News

I used to think it was only Superman who donned a disguise, a secret identity when he wanted to pass as a mere civilian. The other heroes wore masks as part of their colorful crime-fighting getups. "Clark Kent" was a costume. I do the same thing to walk unmolested around town. I like to wear a pair of those clubman frames—half wire, half plastic—with unprescribed lenses. They are like the ones the Colonel wears or Malcolm X or Vince Lombardi. The glasses of space engineers, FBI agents, the barber in

Mayberry. No one takes notice of me. I blend in. Take the Circle Line, the express car to the observation deck, a phaeton around the park. Might as well be invisible. Here I am on a tour of the *New York Times*. I blend. I blend into a Cub Scout troop from Astoria, Queens, all wearing Yankees caps. We go up and down long corridors. Behind these doors, the guide says, are the famous columnists of the newspaper. Murderers Row, she calls it. The composing room is my favorite with its battery of linotype machines, contraptions as large as a small house, with a keyboard springing out the side on a delicate curvy rod and a tiny stool suspended on tinsel nearby. There are signs everywhere ordering us not to speak to the operators who are pulling levers and switching toggles and pounding at the keys like the man behind the curtain in the *Wizard of Oz*. Union rules. It's not like you could talk. The machines belt out a racket as the jointed insect arms bang around in search of the right word. The operators are famously deaf. This is hot type. So deep inside the workings, lead ingots are melting into muddy pools of metal that leak into molds of letters arranged by the machine, line after line, and column after column. It's close in there and the cubs cover their ears. The floor is splattered by frozen sprays of spilled metal. The guide punches my chest and swings the operator around on his springy stool. She draws his attention to my name tag. He spins back to the stuttering machine and pounds a few letters at the keyboard. The machine bucks and snorts, then spits out a slug of crimped-up metal. It reads DEREK SEES TIMES! only it's not that exactly because it's backwards and upside down. Our little group admires the miracle, the little joke that takes this massive pipe organ to play this one tiny note. It is still warm to the touch, minor headline size, a whole story concentrated and condensed into this bite-sized tablet. The cubs crowd around, read the words with their fingers deciphering the message. I want to keep it as a souvenir, but the operator snatches it back and, quick as that, tosses it to a journeyman poking his head out of a hatchway within the sprockets and pulleys. He drops it into the vat of molten lead to be siphoned out as liquid again, into other letter molds forming new letters, new lines, new pages of type that finally is fit enough to print. For a second, the hunk of hard metal floats on the surface of its own melting. The Thing too, I think, puts on a disguise to go unnoticed. A trench coat, slouch hat, and some sunglasses are enough to disappear, even with a bad case of orange skin, into any crowd.

Derek Jeter Derek Jeter Derek Jeter

Every year I change my signature. I'll print. I'll slant it more or make more loops. I'll switch hit, writing in a cramped crabby left-handed, left-leaning scrawl. I have no notion on the effect of the aftermarket for the autographs. Is it even authentic, each new rewiring of my hand? I like to imagine the hubbub in a card shop, a gaggle of collectors squinting, with loupes screwed into their eyes, bent over the memorabilia trying to make sense of the snowflake variations, no two alike. Sure, they've seen the natural evolution of an autograph, its gradual deterioration from some fine example of Palmer Method penmanship to a squiggle and the flourish of an arching line. I only wish I had an "I" so I could change up the dot. Hearts. Circles. I could dot the "j" I guess. Each New Year is a new year for me, always the rookie with a new mark to make. The one I did for H&B was different yet again, block letters like the Eddie Matthews I remember on the old blue-handled Adirondack bat I had in high school, an homage. Truth is I let my mom sign a gross or two of glossies, a bag or two of balls, when I was on the DL, my hand on the fritz. It didn't seem to matter since I forge myself myself. I just think it strange, all the magic locked in that line of ink to actually transform a piece of paper, a baseball, a cap bill into something else again—cash. I think I will try calligraphy this at-bat, bamboo brush and that block of ink I have to wet and mix myself. Hideki took time to study my technique sidelined as he was with his broken wrist. He had me draw a perfect circle. It was hard. "Yes," he said, "now we should consider your breathing." We sat in the middle of centerfield. I held my brush poised ready to become one with the paper. I closed my eyes and felt myself breathe out the me-ness of me. Or so I thought. It wasn't working. I peeked out of one eye. The grounds crew was working quietly around us, raking the infield into lazy wavelike furrows, arranging the bases to look like floating islands. This is all an illusion, I remember thinking. But it didn't take. I sighed and I signed his cast with my 2001 signature, the e's like o's. We bowed to each other and Sensei Matsui said that I should repeat this koan:

Walk when you walk. Talk when you talk. Die when you die.

And I do. I do. After I'm dead, all these scratches I have made will be what's left of me and then, they say, we'll see what I was really worth. Just so many Dereks still in circulation. I think about it. I sign this thing or that thing: a contract, a warrant, a credit card slip, a scorecard, a pennant, someone's belly, hell, my will.

On the Boundary Edge of the Corridor of Uncertainty

The Pakistanis let me sit in on the pickup cricket game at the Great Lawn in the park. They let me play mid on against a right-handed batsman, a kind of shortstop, and a hot spot when the batsman drives through. I'm a golden glove and have a good arm though they'd never let me bowl. The batting in cricket is more like fielding in baseball, using the big flat bat to keep the ball away from the stumps, deflecting it anyway and anywhere you can on the oval. And the game's like dodgeball too, trying to avoid being hit by spinners or going out lbw. I'll admit I have no clue what the hell is going on. I don't know the half of it. And it feels like a very long church service. The match's two innings can take days if everyone agrees. Ali and Ali let me patrol the borders and take tea. The hawks that nest on 5th Avenue launch from their building and ride the rising thermals overhead, flushing pigeons from the museum's eaves. And all of curious New York gathers around passing time. Some hurl Frisbees across the pitch and others toss out baseball chatter—swing batter, swing batter, swing—as a joke. Roller bladers, dog walkers, sunbathers on blankets, joggers, bikers, baby carriages, and folks playing catch or guitar or croquet. Even though it's summer the sun begins to set early, falling behind the row of complicated buildings on the far side of the park. Cricket's crazy, with the pitcher acting more like a runner stealing second and the batter all finesse as he fences with the bouncing ball. Here's the part I like. The umpire is getting out his light meter and taking a reading of the shadows and then shows it to the captain of the team that's up. The ump offers him the light and without any of us knowing the light's all gone. I like that. Offering the light. And then, like that, everyone has packed it in. The lawn's deserted in the dusk. The hawks have been spelled by the chimney swifts and squeaking bats and there are actual crickets limbering up out in the deep trampled grass. They make a mournful kind of chatter or chant. A buggy version of the old Bronx cheer.

Derek Jeter Bangs the Drum Slowly

I've done my share of shoots. But this one is beginning to stink. I try to remember each spring, the team photo days in Tampa where I get to dress in that season's uniforms. The cameras' electronic flashes, singing as they charge up, charge me up. Everything is new. The guy from Louisville is turning bats in the parking lot. There are two dozen mint hats in the locker room boxes. This might be the year I roll my pants legs up or, at least, show some more socks at the ankle. What's this? They've put more cotton in the blend, the fabric breathes better, comes alive. They've shipped Broadway tailors to Florida to do the alterations on the spot. They follow us around with measuring tape, slivers of soap, thimbles and pins, another kind of ancient uniform. The tailors look the same as the ones who work the fashion spreads I do for the men's mags. *Esquire* made me over twice, no, three or four times or more. Here, all evening wear. There, a picnic on a beach. But always tasteful. No birthday suit. I get to keep the clothes. Later, I find out, they airbrushed the stubble on my cheeks and chin, or they airbrushed it in, evened out the skin tone. It's part of the deal. The new me, worked over by art. And every spring the card companies are there taking close-ups with telephoto lenses. They take their turns posing me. Topps needs a headshot and one of me fielding or throwing. I become a living statue. Upper Deck is looking down the barrel of the bat or having me look over my shoulder as I run. I look back at the previous cards, and I like that fresh-faced kid newly hatched each spring. Later, like now, I know how each year turned out. And each year they add another line of stats and the little anecdote about Maria or how my folks never took me to the circus. It begins to accumulate into a kind of life. I like the cards where I am caught in action, floating above the bag or sailing into a stand, defying both gravity and time. A highlight still lit up. But really my favorite card in a pack is the checklist with all the boxes to fill in. I've done that. Check. I've done this. Check. But this, this is new. I am in the dark here, and it is hot. I can't see, and no one out there where they are taking the picture can see me. My uniform is pristine, wrinkle free, but what does it matter? It's a stunt. I've been bagged in sailcloth by Christo and Jeanne-Claude. Captured for all eternity or at least the next ten minutes as "Wrapped Yankee" at the edge of the infield. Negotiations for this have been going on for years. It's part of the piece, I'm told, the negotiations. I'll get a piece of the action on the tail end when the shroud is sold off piecemeal on eBay. They've cinched my waist with a bungee cord. I seem to be tied down like a tent. There is a little play in the fabric and it lufts in the light breeze. But it is hard to move. I can smell the dirt of the infield, my own sweat. It's muffled but Johnny Cash is running through the stadium speakers. It's getting close in here. I'm a ghost, a cocoon, a bag of laundry. Or maybe I am nothing more than a magic trick. When they unwrap me, I'll be long gone, vanished, taken a powder, turned into dust, thin air.

Derek Jeter Calls Off Death

So the ball is falling out of the sky and as it falls I naturally put my glove hand up to block the sunlight but there is no sun. It is New Year's Eve and the only light is the ball itself, Waterford Crystal, all lit from within, descending out of the black backdrop of the sky above One Times Square where I am on the roof, an honorary timekeeper, and I can kind of make out the crowd below counting down, not the numbers exactly, but the pulsing sonic boom of the cadence, and I settle under the sinking ball and wait, pop my mitt a time or two with my fist, recounting how many are out, who's on base, programming in the play after the catch, where my throw should go, to home, a sacrifice fly. There is a reason that batters are so twitchy at the plate, all OCD with the dirt and the buttons and the Velcro straps on the wrist and the lime lines to smudge and the plate to rap with the bat and the spitting and the digging in all designed to ward off the bad magic of the leather-bound, stitched-up, rosin-caked, evil eye aimed at one's skull. One employs any voodoo in that storm. In the field, there is no superstition. It's all skill. But then it happens, it happens sometimes, you just forget what comes, what came, naturally. Forget how to throw. Or more exactly forget how to forget you are throwing. You begin to think about every little fraction inch of motion and it doesn't flow through you. You can kiss it all goodbye. It's like a stroke, like a blown fuse. Knoblauch, Garvey, Mike Ivie. The fear feeds back. You choke. It happens and then you can't get back to the way you were. You can't think your way back to it because thinking is what got you there in the first place. You can't train yourself because you are way overtrained. You go into this dance, this diving spiral, down and down and you can't even begin to imagine the way it was. And the big ball is still coming down and getting bigger as it falls and the air is filled with a snow of old shredded newspapers and new snow snow. Snow that isn't falling but seems to be appearing out of the cold thin air. I can't take my eye off the ball. I've got it, I say. I wave everyone off. I've got it. Mine. It's all mine.

Derek Jeter Saved from Drowning

Just before the latch lets go and the parachute on the parachute drop begins to drop, a gust of wind twirls me toward Keyspan

Park where the Cyclones are up at bat against Mahoning Valley. I've got a blimp-eye view as the ant-like Scrappers turn two. From up here you can see all nine fielders move, a kind of dance routine. Spinning back around, I see the beach below is packed in the way the old photographs liked to show the beach at Coney Island packed. Sardinian. More people than grains of sand, all standing rammed in together as if there isn't anyone left anywhere else in the metropolitan region. They have all come here to the beach to create this strange sweltering infinite mass of foreshortened people, a mad rookery you'd see only on some unnatural nature channel. The thing about those old photographs is that every one of those millions of people on the beach is looking right at the camera, all posed and responding to some little cue to hold it and smile. And that's the way they are now—all looking up at me as I swing on this canvas seat, weightless for a second when the latch lets go and then I begin to fall, floating like a feather. And right away I begin to drift, not straight down directed by the stays and cables, but up and out of the way. I'm getting lift. And down below hands are going up, wave on wave of pointing at my ride on the loose, my chute floating away for the Erector set pylon. Even play has come to a halt in the park below, shrinking in my wake. I'm being carried out to sea by some shore breeze, some shifty trade wind. I'm a Yankee clipper on a reach, running down above the sand, and soon I am out over the water, out past the breaking waves. And the crowd that has tracked me with their pointing, now traces me down down down to the water. I'm not panicked, though I guess I should be. It seems that natural or inevitable. I am caught up in this thing, a big powerless mushrooming poof. What can I do? I tugged a time or two on the guy wires as if I could steer back to the Steeple Chase. And it did take a long time to come back down. I think I forget for awhile that I am falling. But I am falling and fall into the rolling drink, another kind of weightlessness, and above me the huge blue canopy deflates and flattens as it falls into the water after me. I kick out of the harness as the getup sinks and begin to tread water. The crowd off in the distance has crowded up to the water's edge, countless gazes fixed, gazing at me out there bobbing in the brine. There they stand, a huge army, not a lick of space between them, mostly naked in their swimsuits, frozen and in awe at what has just happened. I meekly get out a "Help." That brings them to their senses, and at once the whole endless pack begins to move, running, first, in place for awhile until the front rank goes forward enough to open up some slack like the start of a marathon. And the first wave picks up speed as they are running now into the real waves, the water ones, moving in to meet each other and then out over their heads, the front file begins to dive and swim toward me, the whole beach crawling with bodies pouring into the water, a bog of heads bobbing toward me and all of them all of them wanting to be the one to say they rescued me, wanting to rescue me so much they'd have to kill me to save me. I can feel their good intentions seeping into the soup, washing over me, transmitted through the water, waves of empathy, a kind of fluid affection, the water roiling with tons of love. So I turn right there stretch out and begin to swim toward the open ocean to save who else but myself from all this good intention.

Derek Jeter and the Persistence of Memory

The ballplayers get to tour the Dali Museum for free. We took the freaky four-mile bridge, with its grinning curtain of cables halfway through, across the bay from our camp in Tampa over here to St. Pete, a twi-night doubleheader with the Devil Rays. Al Lang Field's across the street, looking like a melting strawberry cake. The museum is right on the water, and out in the bay. A fleet of caiques bobs, Greek sponge divers waiting to be blessed by an orthodox priest brought over from Tarpon Springs. Most of the team wanders over to have souvlaki served from a pushcart. Nearby is a 24-hour jai alai fronton right next to the largest shuffleboard court in the western hemisphere. The disks tisk softly. Airplanes are already circling for the game. I count ten in the clockwise pattern, hauling banners advertising the new Medicaid prescription plans. Eight more are turning counter clockwise legs, advertising a sun block with SPF of 79. Three blimps. Above it all, a skywriter traces out a smiley face in the severely clear blue sky. I never know how long I should look at a picture before I move on to the next. I stand in a little group before the painting with the melting clocks. The persistence of memory, and pretty soon I sense that I am the one being looked at. The crowd has gathered round. I am in my uniform. That's how they knew to let us in free. I tower over my little cluster, a movable bleacher, and see a similar sight in other parts of the gallery, a Yankee hemmed in by a gazing shuffling flock of civilians. Randy Johnson towers above his crew, is looking at a painting that looks, looking at it from across the room, like a woman one minute then turns into a death-head skull the next if you keep staring at it. I can see we are all trying to figure out when it would be appropriate to move. I do like how the clocks are melting, the one draped over the branch of the tree. The ants on the one clock seem all too familiar as the clutch of fans shifts and sorts around me. I contemplate. I realize that Florida's great gift to the world is ways of waiting. Just simply making the endless lines at Disney World double back on themselves disguised the time it took to wait. The rides are a few seconds. The line to the ride was the real ride after all. Florida is not so much the sunshine state but the waiting state. Baseball, too, is all about the waiting, waiting through the time it takes. Most of all I like the bluff or cliff or mountain off in the distance. It looks so real. I think of what the nun told us in school to help us imagine the eternity we would spend in hell. Imagine a mountain, she said, and every million years a dove flies by, and the endmost tip of one wingtip barely brushes up against the very surface of the mountain for a fraction of a second, rubbing away a microscopic particle of part of a molecule of the mountain, and imagine that the bird does that for the period of time that finally erodes the mountain away, and when that happens, it would be the first half second in the period of time we call eternity. It's time to move, I tell my companions.

SIGMUND FREUD, ALONE AFTER AN INTERVIEW, DREAMS OF QUESTIONS

Can you attach the voice you hear here (the glottal Viennese inflection?), let it vector around this room that is (already?) beginning to arrange itself, knick-knacked and accented, set piece set-dressed in the periphery of your vision? The polished paneling? The wall of books? The winged armchair? And the fainting couch upholstered with tucked and tufted distressed leather, stuffed with (and this is important?) horsehair, a shock of it escaping at the stitched seams? And, did you forget (how could you forget?) to provide the prop of the cigar (always the cigar?), the cigar that is already (already?) present in the mind of the beholder? Me, in the midst of all this this, holding that cigar? The three-piece tweed suit? My elbow on the mantel? The polished wood? The wall of bound (bound?) books? My cigar-shaped fingers tweezing that cigar-shaped cigar? Is there the neatly trimmed beard (always the beard)? And the fob? Is it leaking (slivers of silver?) from what looks like a hemmed incision (under the heart?), (a slit?) in my waistcoat? The watch (inside?) is it time and a symbol (of course?) of time that prompts (that stands for?) hypnosis (prodding memory?)? The watch (its chain?), is it changed into a pendulum? Is the pendulum a crowbar prying into the buried veneers of the past, the de-lamination of time's time, its lamentation? Character, does it derive from the Greek to inscribe or mark (kharakter, karassein?) from (one more scratching?) kharax (pointed, sharpened stick?) a pointed, sharpened stick? Am I, a writer (first?)? A novelist? My cigar-shaped pen, a pen-shaped penis, with it, am I able to transmute sex (say?), into language? Is this your image of me—the reeling out of the language's language? Extracting from the character the character's character? Am I spooling from the patient on the couch, the spooled clew of yarn, a clew of clues? Is that me there, my pen purling, stirring the spontaneous thoughtless thought back down on the patterned paper? Was my greatest character (this invention? this fabrication?) this character named the "unconscious" whose emanations escape, slip out from within, who walks among us? But where does the unconscious reside? Was I a fabricator of imaginary basements built below tracks of apartment flats constructed on vast flood planes? Does this fiction of the unconscious stick? Does this myth (this fiction?) stick? Does this myth I created pass into a kind of reality? Is it not a pen or even penis but more like the dance a needle does teasing out the splinter? Or is it like knitting together skeins of voices we mistake for the waffled, worsted worsting of character, (our own speech?) that constantly surprises us with each emission? Are we (I suspect?) stuffing made of dreams? Is it all in the inflection, the suggestion? Do I stop up the ears with soundings? Do I stuff the throat with voices? Do I poke out the *I*'s with this pointed, this sharpened stick?

BLACK BOX

For awhile there, I was interested in black box narratives. You could send away to the FAA for a transcript or, sometimes, a tape of the actual final words and sounds of the pilots in doomed aircraft. The obscene words, the expletives as they say, were blacked out on the pages or bleeped on the audio. The swearing was epic as the crew headed into a mountain or realized that their plane was disintegrating around them. Often, there would be this other voice, this other character in the drama. It was the airplane itself, producing the warning bells and sirens. At other times those abstract sounds would be digitalized into a voice, that synthetic voice. "Alert!" it would say. "Alert!" And right there on the transcript would be this other voice amidst the final words of the captain and the first officer.

My favorite was the United crash in Sioux City where one of the fan jets on the DC 10 blew up, and the flying turbine blades took out the hydraulics for the control surfaces. They were flying the airplane with the thrust of the remaining two engines alone. The pilots were unable to take their hands from the yoke even though they controlled nothing anymore. The flight engineer, who died I think, ran things with the throttles. "Thank you,

Sioux City. See you on the ground," were the captain's last words as they came in for the crash landing which is so cool as that would be what any pilot would casually say upon getting final routine instructions to land normally.

Flight crews sometimes don't realize they are about to crash. One pilot was talking to his first officer about problems he was having with his wife. He thought she might be cheating on him, running around. It was a real soap opera. They were so distracted they didn't even notice when the plane started talking to them. "Pull up!" it said, "Pull up!" He kept on talking. "Does she still love me, do you think?" And then you heard the copilot say, "What's this?"

Many times the tapes simply end with "Mother!" Honest to God. Or it's "Motherfucker!" or you think it is since the final "Mother...!" has a strikeout trailing it like smoke.

Once, I put a black box on me. I thought I would just record my day. I wanted to forget about it the way flight crews forget it is there. You might be recording your last words but you forget, after awhile, to think of this word as your last word or this one as the last. You go about your business. I had a recorder so light I did forget it was rolling in my pocket.

My tape that day ends with me listening to tapes of black boxes. On my tape you can hear me call to my wife over the cabin traffic recorded on the doomed flight. "Come here," I say, "you have to hear this." You can hear her come in and hear the silence of us listening to the tape of the pilots who are trying to figure out why they are not gaining altitude—turns out they forgot to set their leading edges and flaps. But they don't know that. I say that to my wife, "They forgot to set their leading edges and flaps, but they don't know it." Then, on my tape, you can hear the taped voice of the airplane saying, "Pull up! Pull up!" And then the double silence of my tape and the tape of the black box. And then you hear my wife say, in a voice very much like her everyday voice—not an emergency voice, not a voice of surprise or anger or fear. She says, "Come to bed." And then that's the

GENE STRATTON-PORTER
TRIES ON HATS

Here in Los Angeles, I've taken to wearing a flat cap—herringbone, wool, back to front—the way I've seen the cameramen hereabouts wear them, that stiff brim out of the way as they squint into the viewfinder. Directors, producers too affect them on the set and then dress up as if they are on some kind of safari, all dusty khaki puffy jodhpurs wrapped below the knees with those endlessly winding puttees. Or spats! Gaiters! Chaps! Protection from the snakes all right but not the real ones like those back home in the Limberlost. Vipers, the human kind hereabouts. So that's me too in California all knickerbockered up in the costume of the director and producer I've become. But this getup is more than that for me. I wore it out wearing it out all over Indiana. And I still—between the endless meetings, the take after take of takes, the rushed through rushes—I still like to storm and stumble through the underbrush and bramble of Griffith's Park, the Hollywood Hills, collecting actual racers and rattlers, king snakes and whips. Something real in this made-up make-believe town. Or there are more moths to be had, dolled out in their eveningwear, caught in crowded clouds sapped by the beams of search lit movie openings. Or, still, with my still cameras I capture that shy lazuli bunting in bunting on the wing, that dowager blue bird brooding on her baroque box nest, the tuxedoed chickadee clamoring at some rich under-storied gala.

I've come west to make my books—*Freckles, Girl of the Limberlost, Keeper of the Bee*—into movies. I've liked to see my own books fledge and fluff out into relief, bigger than real life depictions of what had only been dreams, really, tied up in the scribbles I set down over the long, winters in Geneva, at Sylvan Lake. No one knows that the novels, more successful by far than the nature books, were just a camouflage, protective coloration, disguising the real work. Those romances, they made me money, as these movies will too I suspect, to free me up to go outside again each summer collecting.

Pith helmet and sun hat, beekeeper's bonnet and veil, that mattress-ticking engineer's cap, all donned to keep the sun off, to protect me from the elements. My working headgear at times equipped like a miner's with lamp or lantern the better to crawl and climb up into the night or out to the edge of a limb of red oak and hard maple, black walnut and the tulip poplar. You should have seen the rigging I rigged to haul my cameras up onto their perches. The birds seemed to tolerate the awkward gambol of the big format machines. The Brownie scared them. The same scale as predators of the species I suppose. I out Auduboned Audubon, capturing the living animal's image and not articulating the dead. He staged flight while I stopped flying in mid-flap. The only time I was out of the out-of-doors was when I was inside my darkroom, dodging and burning, feathering and folding the light I brought home in a box.

Camera means "room," and I meant to turn indoors inside out, needle the light into the inside and watch as everything knit into lively life. *Friends with Feathers, Homing with the Birds, Birds of the Bible, What I Have Done with Birds.* I liked the way the open books took on the illusion of birds in flight, how each glossy page reflected in its iridescent sheen the robust swirl of shadow and light tangled up in a bird's down, in its telltale tail, its whirlwind of wings whirligigging through the thick Indiana air.

Hats! No one remembers now but hats changed my life. My first published article—"A New Experience in Millinery"—appeared in the magazine *Recreation* in 1900. I could not abide the decoration of women's hats, the plumage and feathers at first, then the posed wing or flared tail and finally then the whole carcass posed, the tortured bodies of birds. Perched upon the platters of brims, dioramas of swallows and swifts, anvil-head dent of a crown, a taxidermy of terns, formaldehyded thrushes, tanned tanagers. Whole blue roosts in Florida of blue herons and egrets were destroyed for an airy feather or two taken from the top of the heads of the magnificent. There were murders of whole murders of crows in order to flock someone's fashionable bowler. The gapping beaks, the curled-up feet went into the scalloped and scaled bands. Back then it just didn't occur to people even with the last of the passenger pigeon gone that there was an end to nature. I suggested that the vanity of feathers might be quenched with the use of ostrich plumes or peacock fan feathers that could be harvested without killing the fowl. And that brings us back to the here and now and the hills overlooking Hollywood and Bel Air where I am building my new house. Griffith once farmed land that is now the park and on his ranch he raised ostriches just for that purpose—to bedeck the superstructure of women's hats. I think of that as I roam the vales and valleys of the Santa Monicas, the old Rancho Los Feliz.

I have a summerhouse too out on Catalina. And there is one more hat I'd like to don, the aviator's, that leather and skullcap lined with fleece. I want to fly, fly out to the island, crewing in the open cockpit of a flying boat. And I want to take my cameras along with me bolted to struts and brackets. I want to fly there beside the big winged condors, the circling ospreys, sidle up to soaring albatross and circling gull and be the first to record that aerodynamic, that warp of wing and nuance of feather. It is not a distance record I seek. Or the altitude or speed. I want to fly beside true flight as close as I could be to this crowning event, this heaven in the heavens.

VERSED

Each examination room has a window, a long narrow window, up high on the back wall near the ceiling, enough to let light in but not to see in if one is standing outside of the building. Outside, the glass is opaque, reflective, and looks like a band of sparkling light in the sun, matte black when overcast, a shadowed slit in the wall of a pillbox. Inside, standing in the examination room, we can clearly see out and not be seen.

*

Our building in the office park butts up against the property line of the backyards of a street of single-family, one-story, clapboard-sided detached houses. The property line, here and there, is planted with ornamental cherry trees (*Prunus cerasus*) that bloom each summer. Again, he is in his backyard again. Male, Caucasian, graying hair and receding hairline (though he often wears a "baseball" style hat), five feet nine or ten, 175 pounds, we'd say. Late 40's, approaching 50 years of age. And we watch him go back and forth, back and forth on his small red-painted "riding mower," the baffled burble of its two-stroke gasoline and oil mixture engine reaching us inside the examination room. His white canvas "tennis" shoes rest flat on the red deck that covers the spinning grass-cutting blades below.

*

On our office walls and on the walls of the office waiting room are numerous framed poster reproductions of portraits painted by Amedeo Modigliani (1884 to 1920), an Italian Jewish painter and sculptor who worked mainly in France. We are attracted to the elongated torsos, the stretched necks, and pale elliptically pointed faces. And we stare at his eyes, the way he renders the eyes, often in the same ovoid shape as the head but also often iris-less, all whites, or a pin prick of a pupil or the eye itself, under a drooping lid, a smudge as if a thumb smeared the details, bruised the paint. No blink. Blank.

*

Versed is a trade name. The drug is known generically as midazolam. It's one of the benzodiazepines and works though the GABA neurotransmitter. We use it, intravenously, for procedural sedation. We need to place the subject in a "Twilight" sleep where we can, while performing the colonoscopy, talk to the semiconscious subject, ask the subject to move or relax or have the subject talk to us. The procedure is "uncomfortable." But Versed creates not only "Twilight" sleep but also, within the subject's temporal cortex's hippocampus and nearby subcortical regions, the inability to create new memories, anterograde amnesia. Versed then is an anesthesia that allows one to feel pain but not to remember feeling the pain. We find it hard to forget, day in, day out. We find we are making new memories all the time, at every moment. And we remember, we think, many memories of the memories we brought with us here from our home though the precise mechanism for storing memories is not well known here. The new memories we have made here have not, as of yet, crowded out the older ones.

*

Our office is in an office park on what was once the outskirts of Fort Wayne, Indiana, but the population of the city has expanded north of the "Bypass," the highway next to which this office park was built in the 1960s. In addition to our gastroenterology office, there is an assisted living facility, a credit union, the public television station with its orchard of dish antennae pointed toward satellites in synchronous orbit low in the southern sky, and the three-building campus of a failed life insurance company campus that then became a "business" school and now rents space to the United States Postal Service as a remote sorting facility. There is a large pond in the middle of the office park, built originally as a reservoir for fire suppression when the park was beyond the city limits but now is just an ornamental pond, surrounded by thirteen weeping willows (*Salix* × *sepulcralis*) randomly planted and of different heights, their trailing curtain of leaves turning yellow in the fall. Squadrons of Canada geese in large low-flying "V" formations vector overhead, land on or near the pond, and range on the grass (*Poa pratensis*) between the buildings and the archipelago of blacktopped parking lots.

*

We watch him as he watches from his seat, riding on his red riding mower, the angling Canada geese as they wheel over our office and the office park. He follows the flock with his head, craning his neck all the time the machine he rides trundles forward, both of his hands steady on the little steering wheel. Perhaps the report of his engine has startled the birds that are not usually startled. Perhaps they are only attempting to aggravate him as they glide and bank then flap their big wings and lift away. We can see they are honking. Their beaks are open and their necks ripple and spasm, but we cannot hear them above the growl of the mower's engine. The grass he is cutting is lush and thick. It has rained. But the small hard rubber wheels of the mower bump and juggle over the uneven ground below the very green grass. The rain has cooled off the neighborhood. He is wearing a red windbreaker made of some kind of plastic, a vinyl probably, that has been imprinted on the back with three big white capital letters: "P," "A," "L."

*

We tell the subjects that we know a great deal about this cancer. We know how fast it grows and how it grows relatively slowly along the wall of the colon. If we do this, we say, we can see it. If we see it, we say, we can do something about it. We say it is a good thing you have come in now. Ten years before the earliest onset of the cancer in your family. As we get older, we say, the wall of the colon becomes effaced, thinner. With someone older, we say, we can be in the middle of the procedure and, suddenly, take a wrong turn, and, what do you know, we are looking at a spleen.

*

William Carlos Williams (1883–1963) was an American poet from the state of New Jersey. He was also a medical doctor who wrote his drafts of his short poems on pages of his prescription pad in his examination office between patients. We have found the size of a blank prescription slip to be just right for us to record these reports from our station here in Fort Wayne in the state of Indiana. It is a widely held belief here that the handwritten prescriptions produced by physicians are unreadable to all but a pharmacist. Our anecdotal musings (we do not dare call them "poems") on our prescription pads go unremarked upon if not completely ignored by the subjects sitting across the desk, distracted as they are by the news we are delivering to them about what we have discovered in their bowel.

*

After hours, as night falls over Fort Wayne, under the cover of darkness, we go up to the roof of our clinic. We keep our telescope there, our antennas and dishes, the microwave receptors, the weather station, and a chaise lounge we got on clearance from Target with a back that raises and lowers in many positions. On the roof, we can stretch out on the chaise and take note of the sky. The nervous chimney swifts scatter and the erratic bats attack the fog of moths and millers hanging around the parking lot lights. The clouds drift silently rearranging themselves like the constantly forgetting subjects on our table. The stars wheel and meteors tumble, burning up before they come anywhere near to hitting the ground. To the north, Evac helicopters hover on approach, inching over the pad on top of Parkview Hospital, where we have privileges, and then land. The moon sets over the Indiana University Branch campus to the west where each July Fourth they launch the fireworks we use to cover the launch of our own courier rockets and stealth satellites. The parking lots below are full that night with folks in lawn chairs or blankets on the lawn, enjoying the show, setting off their own Roman candles, writing their after-glowing names with sputtering sparklers in the dark. Every night, the "Bypass," that bypasses nothing now, is clogged with traffic, a tunnel of light, lights flashing and pulsing, running east to west like the throbbing fiery exhaust trail of a rocket on a curving trajectory already over the horizon.

*

There is an easement that runs between the footprint of our clinic and the back of the lots of the houses next door that allows the utilities to string their wires on wooden poles that are steeped in creosote, a preservative, that in the summer wells up out of the wood, a thick sap. Once, on Earth, the oily tar *Aqua creosote* was used to quell the irritable bowel and detoxify the colon, treat abscesses and ulcers, and even, in small doses, creosote was used as a sedative and anesthetic. We like the charcoal smell of it as we climb the poles using the rungs hammered in the sides of the pole. When they still used landlines, we could tap into the telephones on the wires up there in the crowded cross trees, packed with insulators and transformer tubs and fiber optic cable and electric wires. We listened to the conversations, about weather more often than not, and we could hear the currents, all different voltages humming in the background, harmonizing. We liked to read the history of the splices with our fingers in the dark, the gummy tape and the stripped rubbery insulation, the throbbing current underneath. Amperage spilled from the junction boxes. Ozone perfumed the night. And when we couldn't be seen, we would stand up, slip out onto a sagging wire and walk the distance between two poles, a shadow in the night, lit only by swarms of fireflies that cloaked us further. The insects, for some reason we have yet to ascertain, were madly attracted to us as we balanced there on the wires and cables running through the tops of trees.

*

We can track the going back and forth of the lawnmower long after it has disappeared with its operator around the corner of the house. The violence the blade delivers to the grass one way is reversed when going the other way, the uncut blades lie down differently, reflecting the sunlight in different ways, two shades of green, leaving stripes. We had thought that his going back and forth on his red riding mower was always the same pattern, but now we know there are many patterns he cuts into his lawn. There are yard-long swipes running parallel with the boundaries of the lot. Or they're a kind of chevron bias, scored diagonals. Or he outlines the extreme edge of the lot and then works his way to the center, transcribing smaller and smaller squares, boxes within boxes until, in the middle of the maze, he stops the tractor and lets it idle, a little red dinghy floating in the middle of a green green lake, scalloped waves lapping all around him.

*

In the OR, we have a big red toolbox, mounted on casters for effortless movement, boxy with many sliding drawers, a tool chest made for the garage, the auto repair shop, to store wrenches and ratchets. We got it at Sears. Craftsman. In Recovery a subject is recovering. He is talking with his son who has come to take him home. He says, "Oh thank you for coming to get me. Doctor has another patient at 2:00. There was a bright red toolbox." His son answers him again, "Dad, you have told me that ten times now."

And he has. We tilt our head and regard the drama of remembering. The Versed still lingers in the blood. The declarations are repeated again and again. "There was a bright red toolbox." The son says again, "Dad." He has lost the ability to create new memories. He still doesn't remember what he just remembered to say from before the procedure, before the Versed disabled the mechanism of recollection. We think of the toolbox, bright red, in the next room, its many drawers, the way it glides effortlessly on its casters, all of them able to swivel and turn.

*

Sometimes during our lunch break we dowse. We wander the grounds of the office park, still in our long white medical coats, with a Y-shaped branch we've cut from one of the weeping willows on the bank of the pond. The residents wave from their rocking chairs on the porches of the assisted living facility. Our witching rod trembles in our hands. It is not like we have a pattern, a plan. We are not our neighbor, the mower. Our course over these lawns is much more erratic, random. We let the wand lead us. Or we imagine our imagination is leading us, that we are being led by the wand. A magnetism, a gravity, the willow switch produces or, perhaps, senses. On the lawns, small scrums of geese waddle away, just out of reach, and when the stick shudders quickly, they scatter, flapping their wings and hissing back at us. The rod's motion, its twitching and pecking, Earth scientists feel, is attributed to the ideomotor effect. They believe we believe there is something down there, something below, underground. And, involuntarily, unconsciously the muscles of our arms and hands transmit the movement to the stick. We don't know. We don't know. The residents are amused we think. We wave back and then grab the branch again as if we have almost lost control of it, as if we must wrestle it back under our control. We like the exercise, being led by a stick this way and that. And we do wonder about the archeology of what is unknown, unseen, not sensed, and all that requires instruments and apparatus to detect, to detect. Something.

*

The endoscope has a movable tip and multiple channels for instrumentation, air, suction, and light. The bowel is occasionally insufflated with air to maximize visibility (a procedure which gives one the false sensation of needing to make a bowel movement) but the Versed in the system of the subject creates the inability to remember that particular moment of stimulation or act on it. The air compressor hums softly in the background, a small sneeze when we turn it off or on as we proceed. It hisses like a goose. The quivering image on the screen floats near the ceiling, flickers and fades. The light diffused comes into focus. The colon there blooms open. Slick. Shiny. Scoured.

*

The credit union branch is next to the office park's main entry and egress. They have a drive-through window and after work, on Fridays especially, automobiles line up, curling around the red brick box of a building. We can hear from our clinic's stoop, the pneumatic swallow of canisters filled with checks and cash, the tubes snaking through the rafters above the cars to the tellers in the building. It is often robbed, the credit union branch, having been built that close to the road and the avenues of hasty escapes. The robberies often seem improvisational, opportunistic. Never is much money taken. The robber is always apprehended a few days later or even that same day. Nearby, by the access road, there is a bus stop and a Plexiglas shelter there next to the street that leads to the "Bypass." We often sit there out of the rain, the wind blocked, watching the cars go in and out. A red armored van arrives. A guard, with a gunmetal gun drawn, stands at ease next to the idling truck.

*

There is something about the cant of the head, the way it tilts on the elongated neck. It is like looking into a mirror when we look at the floating frame poster portraits of the artist Modigliani we have arranged on the walls of our clinic's waiting room. They float there at our eye level, over the empty chairs after hours. We never tire of looking, our heads cocked, face to face to face to face. Without turning away, we take a sliding step to the left and shore up again, our right leg following, drawing us up, and stand up to our full height to regard, our head in a list, the next portrait in the gallery. During the day our subjects waiting in the waiting room find the faces comforting, we think. Perhaps it is the faces' pallor or general soothing palette, the soft, shaded almond eyes that don't quite stare, are pleasantly vacant or, more exactly, turned inward or rolled up into the bruised lids in reverie, caught in the gesture of attempting to remember. *Pseudogoitre* of the cervical lordosis is also known as Modigliani Syndrome. All those pleasing ellipses… The swan-shaped neck. We have forgotten if we ever remembered if there ever was one, a mnemonic for its diagnosis.

*

This once was the edge of town, not grain fields as much as wood lots and pasture and unmanaged bottomland along the river, undrained marsh and a played-out stone quarry, all divided up by old dirt section roads and abandoned interurban railbeds. The "Bypass," that now bypasses nothing, swept in a long curve through this wilderness, east to west, a northern arch over the city. The "Bypass" is a parking lot tonight, cars and trucks, stalled in a corridor of ruin—strip malls and dying shopping centers, gas stations and drive-ins. A skating rink, The Roller Dome, one of the first structures to be built on the outskirts, survives somehow, and we can focus on its asbestos-sided lozenge-shaped building with our telescope, see the neon red letters through the light pollution pooling at the clogged intersections. At the end of the road, the "Bypass" is a forest of towers, television and radio, clustered on a cleared glacial drumlin to cheat a few more feet of elevation for the transmissions. We don't need the telescope to pick out the strobing red aircraft-warning beacons, all on different sequences, flashing on and off even as the gantry and the guy wires are invisible in the dark. Two-dozen towers, hundreds of blinking lights levitate, float, hover, disappear, reappear. Nights like this, all those years ago, before the "Bypass," on the edge of town, in the woods, the empty fields, the deserted farm lanes and spoiled hunting blinds, we would search for subjects. We found them too—naked on blankets in clover beds, skinny-dipping in the moonlight in the abandoned quarry, drunk and alone in the back seat of a stalled car stuck in a weed-choked ditch. We were curious. We were curious. And we had ways of making them forget as they opened up to us.

*

It is widely believed that the colonoscopy, the device itself and the procedure, in Japan, by Doctors Niwa and Yamagata in the 1960s. We make no effort to either correct the narrative details of their discovery or dissuade the narrators from relating how the instrument's design appeared to them in a dream. Versed, midazolam, was not patented (US Patent 4166185 issued to Hoffmann-LaRoche), records show, until 28 August 1979, a happy accident of synthesis in the lab of Walser, Fryer, and Imidazo, but who's to say that that particular benzodiazepine didn't exist before then, exist in the wild, so to speak, and might have found its way to be administered, years before, at the isolated Hokkaido research facility of Fujifilm. Fujifilm, to this day, provides the photographic paper on which we print the cross-sectional slices of our interior reconnoitering. We were stationed many years on Ezochi, near the Yunokawa Hot Springs, soaking with the troop of soporific snow macaques in the dead of winter, explorers on that lost remote frontier. There we memorized the renku of the masters Basho (1644–1694), Buson (1716–1784), and Shiki (1867–1902). Here is Issa (1763–1827), our own translation:

ta no hito no kasa ni hako shite kaeru kari

**wild geese take wing
out of the flooded fields
shit on the farmers' hats.**

After a procedure, we sit with the subject as the subject recovers in the recovery suite. We point out, in photograph after photograph, the absence of anything framed by the pink sheen of a clean colon wall. The subject is still under the influence of the drug, Versed, has that *boketto* cast in the eyes, gazing vacantly into a blind distance without thinking.

*

The largest building in the office park was originally built as an insurance company, or to be more exact, a reinsurance company, an insurance company that insures insurance companies. The building is a big glass box, the glass of which is, during the day, reflective, four floor walls of flat mirrors. At night, when lit from within, the building becomes transparent. We can see deep inside the floors, the rows and rows of desks that now, in the night, are occupied with hundreds of workers peering into large monitors on cluttered desks. The insurance company is long gone, replaced by this firm contracted by the Postal Service to remotely decode addresses that machine scanners cannot read. Day and night, day after day, images of indecipherable letters appear on the screens before these data conversion specialists. We watch them at night, not needing our starlight scope to magnify what little available light is available. There is enough light generated from within the building, pouring out the now clear windows. We can read (or not read as that is why the letters are here at this center, for their illegibility) the scribbled addresses on the letters. The letters are scanned in post office distribution centers all over the country and transmitted here to our little office park. Squiggles. Scratch outs. Smears. Erasures. Is that "29" or "2A?" The ghostly letters are like stained specimens on slides under a microscope. It is pathology. This lost mail is on its way to a reconstructed destination or on to a Dead Letter Office somewhere else and a final digital deletion. Millions of villi and the million more of microvilli in the gut increase the surface area of digestion. The mail moves through this office, is handled. The fingers of the clerks blur, typing at their keyboards. The clerks there take turns taking breaks, one at a time. A woman sits in the corner of the building closest to us on the roof of ours. She is alone eating something (a piece of fruit?) we can't quite make out what she has taken from a paper bag. We can see she is enjoying what she is eating. She is eating out of her own hand as she looks into the window that is transparent for us. We can see her. She is enjoying what she is eating. But she cannot see us, see out. Inside the lit-up office, the windows must be like a mirror for her and mirrors her, seeing herself inside the glass building eating something delicious.

*

We determine what is broadcast on the single flat-screen television that floats in the corner next to the ceiling of the waiting room. It is a financial channel that pictures a variety of dynamic graphs—company stock quotations, bond yields, interest rates, commodities markets, futures—rising and falling bright red lines moving left to right, cursors radiating like they are pebbles plopping in a pool. The sound off. The talking heads talk in silence. Ticker tapes crawl, right to left, on the bottom of the screen with news or numbers. The mnemonic for the parts of the bowel is Dow Jones Industrial Average Closing Stock Report: Duodenum, Jejunum, Ileum, Appendix, Colon, Sigmoid, Rectum. We know we should be invested in an Index Fund but instead we invest in individual company stocks, stocks of local companies, so we can read the annual reports and attend the shareholders 'meetings and vote our proxies. Biomet, a provider of replacement joints; Vera Bradley, the bag maker; Tokheim

Pump, a designer of gasoline pumps; and Aardvark Straw Company, the last manufacturer of paper drinking straws in the country.

*

He is wearing some kind of headset as he mows back and forth. Large earphones cover both ears connected by a springy plastic band that reaches over the top of his head, crimping the baseball cap he wears, connecting the two earpieces. The apparatus is not just for sound abatement though it must muffle the riding lawn mower's whiney engine. We know this because both earpieces sprout a single stalk antenna that extends a foot or so over his head. The setup allows him to listen to the radio as he mows. We think it must be one of the talk format stations, one of the stations whose transmission tower is there, blinking, on the horizon at the end of the "Bypass." There are studies that suggest the playing of music during the procedure facilitates the probing, reducing the duration of the procedure and shortening the time in recovery from the anesthesia, the wearing off of the forgetfulness of the Versed. We provide earphones for the subjects, but we also play, through small speakers placed around the room, music we enjoy ourselves. It does make the work go faster. In the past, we often played Dvorak's New World Symphony, the very same recording that Neil Armstrong (1930-2012) took with him to the Moon, which played in the echoing chamber of his helmet while he and Aldrin recovered rock samples during their EVAs. But now we, more often than not, listen to music from the Baroque period, Italian Antonio Vivaldi (1678-1741) being our favorite for now and the Spring movement of The Four Seasons is on repeat. It is on now, and we are waiting for the allusion to the donkey's bray, its big ears of the beast twitching, its body tensed with the exertion of creating the atonal sound. We are also using our parabolic dish to attempt to discover the whisper in the ear of the mower as he mows back and forth, the antenna like conductors' wands. It is probably a sports discussion, the talk he is listening to, the chances The Fighting Irish of Notre Dame will have for the coming season.

*

The roots of the willow aggressively seek sources of water below the ground. The weeping willows produce an extensive system of shallow roots that extend out from the trunk and beyond the canopy of the tree, reaching more than one hundred feet in all directions. Horticulturalists suggest that the trees be planted in the open away from underground waterlines, agricultural tile, or sewers of all sorts, as ours are there next to the pond where the silver green foliage of the bending branches seems to be admiring their own reflection in the water below. The mower in the backyard of the house adjacent to our office seems to mow his lawn constantly. The swaths of lawn stretching out between the buildings of our office park are mowed as well but not as often by gangs of landscape maintenance men who steer donkey engine mowers, like dogsleds, standing behind the motor and the blades on a gliding platform as they maneuver. One day we look up from our reading or from our annotation of a specimen or in the middle of the procedure to see two, three, four, or more of these tractors traveling in all directions, their pilots, tall upright, floating over the leafy grass. At night, the nozzles of the underground irrigation system emerge and begin to distribute the water in misting clouds. The ground hugging shadows of geese drift toward the copse of sprinklers that is engaged and when those shut off they turn toward the fresh spring one field over.

*

Oh, Oh, Oh To Touch And Feel A Girl's Vagina, Ahhhh, Heaven. Olfactory, Optic, Oculomotor, Trochlear, Trigeminal, Abducens, Facial, Auditory, Glossapharyngeal, Vagus, Accessory, Hypoglossal. The twelve cranial nerves. Our favorite is the number ten, the Vagus nerve, the wanderer—the vagrant, the vagabond, vague. It wanders parasympathetically sprouting from the brain, the medulla oblongata, down through the neck, chest, abdomen where it contributes to the innervation of the viscera all the way to the colon where it is responsible for the task of gastrointestinal peristalsis and the seat of our study. Sweating, heart rate, speech, the gag reflex, and why one might cough when the ear is cleaned by a cotton swab—the gangs of ganglia of the vagus nerve descending. Vasovagal syncope is the most common cause of fainting, a dysfunction of the regulation of the heart and blood pressure in response to an emotional trigger such as the sight of blood, say, or watching or participating in a medical procedure. A person is predisposed to this response and it probably survives in the minority of the population after ancestors on some battlefield were disposed to faint and lived by appearing to be dead. Playing possum written into wiring. Like the sad-eyed possums (*Didelphis virginiana*) we watched foraging as we waited above the clearings in the dark woods. We recorded the symptoms of syncope in our subjects as our sudden appearance before them stimulated the vasovagal response—lightheadedness, nausea, hot or cold sweating, ringing in the ears, an uncomfortable feeling in the heart, fuzzy thoughts, confusion, a slight inability to speak or form words, mild stuttering, weakness, lights seeming too bright, fuzzy tunnel vision, black cloud-like spots before the eyes, and nervousness, general nervousness. And then the fainting. The unconsciousness.

*

The preparation, we agree, is as uncomfortable, if not more uncomfortable, than the actual procedure. The colon must be free of all solid mater. Sodium picosulfate, sodium phosphate, magnesium citrate and large quantities of fluid rich in electrolytes. The regime focuses the attention inward. Rarely does one register the sheets of muscles rippling beneath the skin with such clarity. It is, we have been told by subjects, as if there is something alive inside their lives. There is too another kind of nakedness, an undressing of modesty the subject inhabits as the chemicals turn the body inside out.

no setchin no ushiro wo kakou yanagi kana

**impromptu outhouse,
what to screen my bare ass
the lone willow**

Issa again. We walk the grounds of the office park waiting for the day to begin. Everywhere in the green grass there is the green shit of geese.

*

In the days that Dr. Williams was writing his notes in his examination room on prescription pads between patients, he would be the first to tell you that it is all about diagnosis. It is not so much about the treatment or the cure, but all about the careful collection of histories and samples, the scrupulous cataloging of gestures and anatomies. We can see the residents of the assisted living facility rocking on their sun porch, see the way morning light falls upon them at the speed of light, falling on the fraying wicker of their chairs and staining their skin. They are looking right at us. Do they remember us from the day before, or the day before that, do you think? The orderly, behind them is framed in the screen door, is cut in half by solid shadow. His scrubs are white, but look gray, and he is looking at a phone held in his palm of his right hand. The only thing moving is his thumb, scrolling on the screen. The dew on the grass at our feet evaporates. We see the drops of water on the blades of grass, and then we don't.

*

Above the mini-refrigerator in the break room is Modigliani's *Nu Couché de Dos.* The composition of the female subject is not unfamiliar to us. The eyes are not only almond shaped but look, if you look closely at them, like smooth rust-colored almonds. They are iris-less, unfinished, and scored with marks of scarification found on the surface of a seed or pit. Oil on canvas, 99.5 cm x 64.5 cm. The splayed legs extending into the lower right corner create a V-shaped negative space, filled by the deep red of the cushion she rests upon. She looks at us, not over her shoulder, but wedged beneath the arch of the shoulder's curve. Her head rests on her pillowing hand and her chin is tucked in under the shoulder. That hand on her cheek, that soft shoulder create another V-shaped space there, the red cushion peeking through between the flesh-colored flesh. In the refrigerator, we keep fruit. Plums and peaches, Michigan cherries in a blue ceramic bowl. Apricots and nectarines. Salty olives, that we prefer cold. The bramble berries on a white dish—blackberries and raspberries. Stone fruit. Drupe. Drupe, whose seeds are designed to pass through you. We are sorry that the painting we have in the break room is the real painting. Not a reproduction. Long ago now, we took it from the Barnes in Lower Merion, Pennsylvania. We left a note, a note apologizing for its absence, saying it was on tour or undergoing restoration. We are not sure. We can't recall.

*

The sun setting and the Canada geese have taken flight in ragged "V" formations, spiraling up away from the pond and circling the park in search of other open fields now that this one is over-run by people parked here for the fireworks. Some of the birds have taken to the pond, floating there forming a honking raft in deeper water away from crowds and cars. We are on the roof of the clinic readying our own rockets, attaching their payloads. In our practice we do use, from time to time, capsule endoscopy, that little pill with the tiny camera to travel the length (nine meters, 30 feet) of the gastrointestinal tract, all the time transmitting images of the journey and tracking its progress in real time wirelessly. These rockets here on their launching pads, we think, are like that. It is all a matter of scale. They will be swallowed into space. Humans sitting on blankets blanket the open spaces for as far as the eye can see. The stars begin to open, one by one, in a sky more clearly black now that the sodium lights of the parking lot and the arch lights of the "Bypass" and the neon signs of the businesses have been extinguished for the occasion. The residents of the assisted living facility are in their rockers on their porches asleep and dreaming. They will miss nothing that they haven't seen before. The ornamental trees along the property line are filled with small children who have climbed up into them, curled up, and are cradled in the branches. Through the now transparent windows of the remote mail office, a few monitors flicker on overtime, tiny in the distance, postage stamps in the window frames. One, we see, now that we have brought the telescope to bear, displays jumpy pornographic imagery—a penis entering into and withdrawing from an anus—the human in the penumbra watches, reflecting, the head tilted. The first of the fireworks goes off. We feel it before we see it. The launching mortar makes a deep thump that resonates in our gut, and we catch, out of the corner of our eye, the firework rocket ascending through ground fog, a snaking sporadic exhaust signature and then the spherical burst in three dimensions but what always reads as expanding in the flatness of two, the boom of the dispersal following, an afterthought to the shimmering sparkle already dissipating, the ghostly cloud of the spent explosive already drifting west, giving us our calculation of windage. We finish our preflight protocols, top off the fueling, set telemetries, download data—all the time single bombs and paired flares ignite in our background, showering sparks in all colors, making targetable concentric circles, halos inside of holes, the countless glittering specks another kind of gut flora. We are waiting for the finale, the barrage of missiles and rockets, the cascades of light that open inside one another and the single flashes of the bombs that transport nothing more than a blinding burst of sound. Then and there, we will launch our own homely projectiles into and through the clutter of pyrotechnic camouflage. Onboard, another chapter of our ongoing exploration, our findings, though we cannot remember, if we ever really knew, what we were sent here for and what we were meant to find.

TEST PATTERN

Philo T. Farnsworth, the inventor of electronic television, on his knees. Philo T. Farnsworth, the inventor of television, on his knees in his living room. Philo T. Farnsworth on his knees in his living room watching the television. Philo T. Farnsworth on his knees before the television in his living room. Philo T. Farnsworth, the inventor of TV, on his knees in his living room, in the house, on State Street, in Fort Wayne, Indiana. Philo T. Farnsworth, the inventor of television, regards the TV. On the television is the test pattern. It is late at night. It is early in the morning. The test pattern is being broadcast on NBC. The test pattern is being broadcast on CBS. The test pattern is being broadcast on ABC. Philo T. Farnsworth switches the television from NBC to CBS to ABC. NBC, CBS, ABC are all broadcasting the same test pattern. NBC, CBS, ABC have all signed off for the day. Signing off, the broadcasters broadcast the broadcasters' daily recital of the Television Code. After the recitation of the Television Code. After the recitation of the Television Code. After the recitation of the Television Code, NBC, CBS, ABC have played the National Anthem. The National Anthem is accompanied by pictures. As the National Anthem plays the broadcasters broadcast pictures. They each run a film while the Nation Anthem plays. On NBC a formation of United States Navy jets (The Blue Angels) flies above a fleet of United States Navy ships. On CBS a formation of United States Air Force jets (The Thunderbirds) flies in formation over the Grand Canyon. On ABC a formation of silver jet bombers (The Strategic Air Command) flies over nothing, flies over nothing Philo T. Farnsworth can see, filmed simply as they fly in what must be a blue sky but looks on television to Philo T. Farnsworth like a gray sky, not white and not black. The contrails of all the jets. The contrails of all the jets as they fly. The white contrails of all the jets as they fly through the gray sky are white parallel lines streaming behind the jets in formation. The white parallel lines of the jets' contrails remind Philo T. Farnsworth. The white parallel lines of the jets' contrails remind Philo T. Farnsworth of the 525 equally spaced lines of fluctuating light that create the picture of white parallel lines of exhaust now dissipating against the background of gray sky as the end of the National Anthems is broadcast. Then the screen grows dark. The screen grows dark. The screen grows dark before the test pattern appears. The test pattern appears. The test pattern appears. The test pattern appears accompanied by a 1kHz test tone. The test tone is 1kHz. The test tone that accompanies the test pattern is broadcast continuously at 1kHz. Philo T. Farnsworth, on his knees in front of the television, late at night, early in the morning, regards the test pattern. There is a circle in the upper left-hand corner of the screen. There is a circle in the upper right-hand corner of the screen. There is a circle in the lower left-hand corner of the screen. There is a circle in the lower right-hand corner of the screen. In the circles. The inside of the circles is inscribed with crosshairs of fine lines shading to thicker lines, with scales of numbers 20-25-30-35, and parentheses inside parentheses, the arch they transcribe congruent to the radial arch of the enclosing outer circle. The four circles (each tangential) touch at four different points, a larger circle, its very black circumference circling the center of the screen, its center circled by another circle and still another circle closer to the center and, inside that inside circle, rings of circles, each ring inside the one before and outside the one after, decreasing in diameter, until, at the very center of all the circles and rings the number 30 which is also the middle number of another scale of numbers running through the inner circle of the inner circle on the diagonal, SW to NE, 20-30-30-45-35, which are themselves dissected by the pulsing parentheses seen in the smaller outer circles, the parenthesis like residual circles, ruins of other circles, lost orbits of other test patterns, suggestions of the pulse of electromagnetic radiation expanding outward from the point where the electromagnetic radiation originally emanated. Philo T. Farnsworth, the inventor of electronic television, on his knees in front of this television, adjusts the picture being produced by this television using the test pattern as a test pattern. There are rays of lines, rays of shades vectoring from the center of the circle or circles. Lines splay as they move farther from their points of inception. Lines grow thicker, wider, darker, lighter. Philo T. Farnsworth, on his knees, adjusts his television to the tune of the 1kHz test tone. He whistles in harmony as he works. Philo T. Farnsworth fiddles with the knobs below the screen. The knob that adjusts the vertical. The knob that adjusts the horizontal. The knob that adjusts the contrast. The knob that adjusts the brightness. Behind the screen, in the picture tube, the picture tube Philo T. Farnsworth invented when he invented television, is a 25,000-volt electron beam being bent and directed by the calibrations of coiled electromagnets analogically connected to the knobs being manipulated by Philo T. Farnsworth in his living room. The knobs are necessitated by the vagaries of trying to deflect a 25,000-volt electron beam shot 60 times per second into 525 equally spaced lines of fluctuating light against the inner, phosphor-coated surface of a glass tube. Philo T. Farnsworth brings the test pattern into focus. Philo T. Farnsworth brings the test pattern into focus. Philo T. Farnsworth brings the test pattern into focus. Philo T. Farnsworth brings the test pattern into focus. The test pattern is a standardized image used for the adjustment of vertical and horizontal linearity (proportions), scanning linearity (even spacing of the scanning lines), video frequencies (shading), picture detail resolution (focus), interlacing and oscillation, both at the center of the screen and at the corners (where performance is most likely to degrade). The circles. The shadings. The grids. The diagonals. The converging lines. The diverging lines. There is also the image of an Indian. There is an image of an Indian, not quite in profile, not quite full-face. There is an image of an Indian, an Indian in a full-feathered headdress. Philo T. Farnsworth regards the image of the face of the Indian. Philo T. Farnsworth regards the face of the Indian as he focuses the face of the Indian in the test pattern. The representation represented by the face of the Indian is in stark contrast to the other images on the test pattern. The cameo of the Indian floats amidst the field of the other graphics, the other more technical graphics of the test pattern. The image of the Indian is organic. The image of the Indian is asymmetrical. The image of the Indian alludes to a third dimension that the scanned lines of the television can only suggest. A depth. A roundness. Philo T. Farnsworth directs the scanning beam of electrons to stimulate the phosphors of the screen to simulate the fibers of each feather of the headdress, the cant of the muscle and cheek bone under the skin of the Indian's face. Philo T. Farnsworth adjusting his television set focuses on the eye of the Indian, the left eye (the one he can see) with its concentric circles of eyelid, iris, and pupil. Philo T. Farnsworth sees this eye come in focus, sees this eye focus, its pupil dilating, adjusting to the light. Philo T. Farnsworth feels his own eye dilating as he inches his face up toward the face of the Indian on the test pattern. Philo T. Farnsworth feels his eye scan the surface of the screen as the screen is scanned 60 times a second by the 25,000-volt electron beam that he invented, that he is now (this night, this early morning) deflecting, deflecting to bring the test pattern into focus. Nothing is moving except the incremental modulations of light and darkness. Nothing is moving but the muscles in his eyes, the muscles in his fingers. The test tone of 1kHz is the only sound. Philo T. Farnsworth has all night. Philo T. Farnsworth has all morning. Philo T. Farnsworth has all night, he has all morning to test the test pattern, to get it almost right, to get it just right, to get it nearly right, to get it right, to get it, to get it right, to get it, to get, to get it too.

MM + MM + MM + MM

FOOTNOTES IN SEARCH OF A STORY

[23]MM directing the attention of her colleagues at the *Scuola Ortofrenica* to observe the "unhappy little one" as he sweeps sand into a dusty pile on the floor says, "A child's play is his work."

[12]MM in the Pyrenees, banished by Mussolini, walking the *Camino de Santiago de Compostela*, toys with the scallop shell in her pocket still gritty with some sand of Anzio.

[c]MM snorts when the ump, having called time, steps over the plate, the whisk broom already taken from its pocket in the chest protector, points his butt toward centerfield, bending over to sweep home clean, farts a little but enough to be heard even with all fan hubbub in the air all around.

[n]MM peels through the pages of his raft, the spell book, looking for an incantation in the vortex of the flood brought on by a phalanx of brooms.

[?]MM sweeps in the corners of the kitchen after dislodging a green plastic sniper draped in a ghillie suit of cobwebs.

[9]MM, out after curfew, looks up through the crisscrossing

wrought iron of the fire escape latticed on the backside of the Hotel Cadillac and sees the zipper of his initials.

ᵏMM on deck, the bad knee he has taken in the circle grinds into something buried in the dirt, a lead ballplayer, a batter swinging two bats, in pinstripes no less.

ʸMM at a table in the middle of nowhere with Whitey where Michael Martone's father finds him and asks him for an autograph for his son who is named Mick too.

πMM, asleep, dreams he is commanding the stars that disintegrate as they fall from the sky, the light of their phosphorescent tails gritty with sparkle.

ωMM looks up sheepishly at the sorcerer, shrugs, his shoulders making valleys and peaks, edges by his master who then swats MM on his backside, sliding him to the door.

↗MM's son, met at the door by his teacher, tells her today he would like to play in the kitchen, and she shows him where the brooms are kept.

⌘MM, right-handed, his son left-handed, oils the gloves with the neat's-foot oil and then, snapping a glove on each hand, scuttles across the beach to play catch.

θMM trapped in the folds of his master's gown, the declivities and crevasses, peeking from beneath an avalanche of cloth, his peaked cap a peak, reflecting the stars.

≙MM's son at the sand table has already uncovered the pig and the dog, the pan and the ring and placed the objects on the words, but he is still looking for the man, the man still buried in the sand.

[44]MM, in The Netherlands, mucks through the mud behind the dike, unearthing the delftware shards there as the sails of the mills above creak and lift, lift and creak.

[♦]MM watching his son deploy his army of army men on the kitchen floor allows the video camera to record the four-hour unfolding battle.

[127]MM meets the *carabinieri* in the doorway of the *Casa dei Bambini*, asking them what they wanted to do today, the perennial greeting, over their barked orders of exile.

[mm]MM circles under the M&M Roger has popped up outside the bodega, losing it in the zigzag girders of the elevated, the 4 train rattling overhead.

[ε]MM, with the ax in shadow, splits the broom handle, hacks the broom and buckets into kindling, chips and wedges, fly into splinters.

[m]MM's son carries a bucket of soapy water to the far end of the classroom, throwing the hard yellow sponge toward the window.

[87]MM on the *Afsluitdijk* washes a sketch of the diminished waves of the *Zuiderzee*, now the *IJsselmeer*, with a diluted phthalo blue.

[t]MM that afternoon before the game in Enid, Oklahoma, went into a movie house to get out of the heat, watched *Fantasia* off and on, and that night, shattered his bat playing a half-assed game of pepper warming up.

[❀]MM in an office building in Fairbanks watches a raven on the flat roof of a building below roll a snowball with its beak to the edge above the door and drop it on someone's head below.

^λMM tries to stop the parade of animated brooms marching down the stairs rank on rank, a rally of fascists, their buckets of water sloshing balletically.

[⊠]MM, waiting in a line for a ride at Disneyland, realizes that this waiting, this line folding back and forth on itself, is a kind of game, a dance, and so constructed that he forgets, finally, that he is waiting but instead feels that whatever he had been waiting for has already started to happen long ago.

⁵⁰MM in Jodhpur observes langurs scratching the rooftop pebbles into dusty piles that other langurs take apart, stone by stone, looking under each as if something has been hidden there.

ⁱMM, from the dugout, watches Mickey Mouse dressed in an Angels' uniform, a glove on over his gloved hands, wind up and throw the first pitch into the dirt.

[•]MM in his car shadows his son's yellow bus on its way to Montessori school, playing tag with the headlights, flashing them at his son looking out through the windows of the emergency door.

⁹MM attends Stokowski conducting the Royal Philharmonic Orchestra performing Rimsky-Korsakov's "Scheherazade" where the children accompanying her fall asleep in clumps on the floor of the loge.

[≋]MM plays catch with his son not noticing it is the ball his father gave him signed by Mickey Mantle until, missing a throw,

he picks the ball up out of the dirt, the sutures of the seams razz red m's.

✱MM's son sweeps the classroom floor every afternoon before dismissal and every afternoon he discovers in the fine ash of dust a treasure of lost manipulatives.

AUTHOR'S NOTE

Michael Martone was born in Fort Wayne, Indiana, and went to the public school there, attending North Side High School during the years they took to renovate the old building. The construction went on all four years of Martone's time in high school and the students worked around the workers who closed first one wing of rooms then the next, sending classes looking for a new space or reclaiming a room now rewired or freshly painted or floored with new terrazzo. The electricity for the master clock in the principal's office had been cut early, and all the clocks in the hallways and classrooms found their own separate times. Most stopped. Some sped up, swept ceaselessly, or stuttered in place as if it was now impossible to move to the next second or the next, sticking with each tick, mesmerizing Martone with a cruel montage of what was now becoming his lost and wasted youth. The period bells, the commencement and dismissal bells, had quit ringing months ago, and the space of time when the students changed classes was marked in gritty silence. A rudimentarily PA system had been jerry-rigged, tinny speakers and exposed wires, and each morning the Guidance Counselor squeaked that the official North Side time was whatever it was. Everyone set his or her watch, regulated for the rest of the day, shuffling through the debris and drop cloths in the work-light lit hallways. It was here Martone first studied chemistry in the 50-year-old laboratories on the third-floor east wing that would be the last to see repair. He still has his slide rule, Army surplus, in its leather case. The hairline cursor embedded in the sliding glass indicator, he realized, was a real hair. He learned to manipulate the contraption in the oversubscribed extra credit slide rule seminar after the regulation lab session. There, too, in the chemistry labs, he saw, for the first time, his teacher perform the Old Nassau clock reaction. He mixed the solutions in the big Pyrex beaker to first produce a pumpkin orange precipitate as a mercury compound settled out and then, after several seconds, the bright orange suddenly turned to a liquid lamp-black as the excess iodine leftover transmuted to starch and turned on its color, a black black curtain dropping instantly. The demonstration was meant to astound with its alchemy, and Martone was astounded, asking to see again the chemical logic of it, how benign soluble concoctions created a product that became a new reactant that then was ready to react. He liked both the anticipation and the rapidity of the transformations, the visual demonstration of whole moles being stewed in their own molecular juices, the quick switch and then its double-cross. It was called a "clock" because of the predictable ticking of the bonding and unbonding that time out perfectly, a collection of ionic seconds spinning on their own internal clocks. This led to this and that to this. The equal sign is replaced by arrows in a chemical reaction, one thing after the other. Years later, when he was a senior in organic chemistry, Martone asked the teacher if he could, in his spare time, work on constructing a new clock reaction that would, this time, express itself in North Side

High School's colors, red and white, not out of any school spirit but mainly out of an urge to tinker with the watch-works of cooked-up nuclei and electron shells. After all, the class he was taking spent its time knitting together long compounded chains of carbons and hydrogens and oxygens, matrices of esters and ethers, another kind of ticking, the proteins twisted into the worsted zipper of a gene undergoing mitosis, another two-step through time. In that lab, too, he set a girl's hair on fire with the Bunsen burner, the flame eating up the long straight strands of her long brown hair like a fuse, another illustration of time. The burned hair, turning to ash, flaked, crumbs of a rubber eraser, spilling to the floor as the stink of it, the hair burning, rose in almost visible solid cartoon waves of wavy stench, the glow of the actual burning peeling now in the nape of her neck, the instant chemical reaction of it, giving off its own unique rainbow of bright colors. They had been performing primitive, spectral analysis, igniting unknown compounds held in little wire loops over the lip of flame, reading the combustion's signature through the slit of a cheap prism tube. The tip of her hair sparked as Martone tipped the burner toward, what turned out to be, a sulfuric something or other. Martone damped down the crawling flicker with his hand, his fingers flouncing the hairs that wove themselves into a now ratted cap, a nest, and for a moment it seemed that the whole canopy would ignite, enriched by the addition of fresh air. Martone was left holding this halo of fire, a hat from hell, a melodrama of oxidation, when, just then, the teacher pulled them both in to the emergency shower where they were doused and, just as suddenly, engulfed in wet smoke and sodden hairy ash. Martone never did find the combination of compounds to create the clock reaction in his school colors. He remembers pouring through old manuals his teacher gave him with pages of tables listing reactants and products and their shades of colors, valences and radicals, ions and elements, metals and base. He wandered through the old laboratory's closets looking for odd specimens in ancient glass bottles stopped up with moldy cork or decaying rubber stoppers, the forgotten chemicals undergoing their own unsupervised and unrecorded experiments, reactions oxidizing into clumps of rusty rust, bleached stains, inert crystalline sweating salts, the paper labels foxing, the beakers mired in viscous goo, and the wood racks gnawed at by some now long gone acidic lick. Helping to clean out the closets in anticipation of the renovation, Martone garnered extra credit to offset the disappointment and possible average grade for his disappointing independent study. In the mess he found the apparatus used through the years to create the famous Old Nassau clock reactions for succeeding classes—the tinctures of iodine, the compounds of starch, the granules of potassium, and the etched graduated cylinders set to deliver the proper quantities of chemical ingredients for the demonstration of time all that time ago. Years later, Martone is on the phone to his classmate from those years whose hair he set on fire during an experiment meant to identify certain chemicals by the spectrum of light they emit when set on fire. Martone has taken to looking through his past lives, has found many of his former classmates by employing the emerging electronic technologies online. He lives now far away from Fort Wayne, in Alabama, and finds it difficult to return home for the sporadic reunions, and when he does, others from back then now live even farther away or seem to have disappeared altogether. He thinks of it as a reconstitution, as hydration, this telephoning, and admits that his efforts redoubled after the collapse of the towers in 2001. That collapse seemed to be a kind of boundary, a membrane, a demarcation as narrow and fine as the hair fused in glass on his slide rule, of before and after. He found her, the woman whose hair he set on fire in his high school chemistry lab, living in New York teaching organic chemistry, of all things, at Columbia University there. The irony was not lost on them. She explained to him that she now was attempting to isolate low-molecular-weight chromium-binding substance in human urine. It had something to do with diabetes and insulin and iron in the blood. It was late at night and they had been talking on the phone for awhile about the past and chemistry and what they had both been doing separately at the same time during all those years when suddenly Martone heard band music. It was past midnight. The music, even diminished by the telephone, was distinctively brassy and rhythmic, shrill and thumping. Martone identified it as "The Horse," a favorite of their own high school's pep band years before. "Oh that," she said. "It's Columbia's marching band. A tradition. They spontaneously appear on the night before the orgo final and march around the Upper West Side." No one will believe this, Martone thinks. After all these years, no one will believe such coincidences of time and space. He learned long ago in the sciences classes of his high school that there were these things called constants. Gravity was one. The speed of light, he remembered. And time—time was constant too.

ACKNOWLEDGMENTS

Allow me to thank all of the editors of the following magazines and journals and acknowledge the aid and comfort afforded to me and these virulent fabrications and fictions.

"The Moon over Wapakoneta" first appeared in *Crazyhorse*.

"The Digitally Enhanced Image of Cary Grant Appears in a Cornfield in Indiana" appeared itself online at *Knee-jerk* and later manifested itself on a placemat in *Paper Placemats*, edited by Paul Maliszewski for J&L Books in 2004.

"The Man's Watch" first appeared online at *Diagram*.

"Anton Chekhov Writes to His Friend, William Sydney Porter, in the Columbus, Ohio, Federal Penitentiary" first appeared in *Zone 3*.

"Seven Flag Days" was published anonymously in *The New Anonymous*.

"Alonzo Reed, Dictating to His Collaborator, Brainerd Kellogg, Loses Track of What He Was Thinking Only to Notice His Audience Is, Already, Lost in Thought" appeared first in *Iron Horse Literary Review*.

"A Bucket of Warm Spit" appeared in *Midway* and was collected in *My Mother She Killed Me, My Father He Ate Me*, edited by Kate Bernheimer and published by Penguin in 2010.

"App ro x i m ate" first appeared in *Copper Nickel.*

"A Convention of Reanimated William Faulkners" manifested first in *Oxford American* as "Viral Free-Floating Critical Commentary."

"Four Yearbook Signatures" may be found online at *Crashtest.*

"Amish in Space" may be found in *J+L Illustrated.*

"*The Blues of the Limberlost* by Vladimir Nabokov: Reviewed by Michael Martone" first appeared in *The Official Catalog of the Library of Potential Literature*, edited by Ben Segal and Erinrose Mager for Cow Heavy Books in 2011.

"Four Hundredth Forty-fourth Night, Give or Take" first appeared in *Waxwing.*

"The 20th Century" may be found online at *Gulf Coast.*

"*Kodak: The Film*: Reviewed by Michael Martone" may be found online at *TROP.*

"Key" first appeared in *Parakeet.*

"The Death of Derek Jeter" was commissioned by Tom Chiarella, editor extraordinaire, and appeared first in *Esquire* in 2009.

"Sigmund Freud, Alone after an Interview, Dreams of Questions" appeared first in *Dislocate.*

"Black Box" first appeared in *Mid-American Review.*

"Versed" was discovered first in *StoryQuarterly* 51.

"Test Pattern" appeared first in *Parcel*.

"MM+MM+MM+MM: Footnotes in Search of a Story" first appeared in *Fugue*.

"Author's Note" first appeared as "Contributor's Note" in *Quarter After Eight*.

Copy that, FC2 Mission Control: Dan Waterman, Lou Robinson, Lance Olsen, Rachel Levy, Joanna Ruocco, Michael Meija, Noy Holland, and all the Crew at FC2 and the University of Alabama Press.

Calling Planet Alabama: Robin Behn, Wendy Rawlings, Joel Brouwer, Kellie Wells, Heidi Lynn Staples, Hali Felt, L. Lamar Wilson, John Estes, Fred Whiting, Deborah Weiss, Heather White, Emily Wittman, Yolanda Manora, Albert Pionke, William Ulmer, Patti White, Karen Gardiner, Brian Oliu, Nathan Parker, Tasha Coryell, Kevin Waltman, Jessica Kidd, Eric Parker, Trudier Harris, Phil Beidler, John Crowley, Bruce Smith, Joyelle McSweeney, Kate Bernheimer, Lex Williford, Dave Madden, Peter Streckfus, Lucy Pickering, Andy Johnson, Mindy Wilson, Kathy Merrell, Bill and Bebe Barefoot Lloyd, Leslie and Dan Hogue, Grace Aberdean, Jason McCall, Jeremy Butler, Frannie James, Melissa Delbridge, Charles Morgan, and Sandy Huss.

Time Travelers: Joe Geha and Fern Kupfer, Steve Pett and Clare Cardinal, Sam Pritchard and Tista Simpson, Susan Carlson, Rosanne Potter, David Hamilton, Kathy Hall, Mary Swander, Susan Carlson, Jane Dupuis, Rick Moody and Laurel Nakatdate, Chris Riley and Mark Feldman.

Celestial Navigation: John Barth, Scott Sanders, Edmund White, Dana Wichern, Howard Junker.

Four Visible Moons of Jupiter: Tessa Fontaine, Jess Richardson, Betsy Seymour, Dara Ewing.

The Shooting Stars: Jim Merrell, Hobson Bryan, David Allgood, Sam Rombokas, Bob Lyman, Mirza Beg, Jim Labauve, Steve Davis, Bill Buchanan, Lee Pike.

Solid Fuel Boosters: Rachel Yoder, Jenni ver Steeg, Colin Rafferty, Elizabeth Wade, Jennifer Gravley, Matt Dube, Miles and Susan Gibson, Michael Czyzniejewski and Karen Craigo, Del Lausa, Vivian Dorsel, Lauren Leja.

Planet Indiana: B.J. Hollars, Deborah Kennedy, Meg Paonessa, Julia Meek, Dawn Burns, Linda Oblack, Sarah Jacobi, Dan Zweig, Jill Christman, Mark Neely, Jean Kane, Patty Brotherson, Kathy Curtis, Lynn Cullen, Linda Dibblee, Andy Payne, Irene and Robert Walters, Wayne and Ruth Payne.

My Mercurys: Sean Loveless and Peggy Shinner.

North Star: Marian Young.

Particle and Wave: Susan Neville, Michael Rosen, Jay Brandon, Michael Wilkerson, Ann Jones, Melanie Rae Thon, Nancy Esposito, Rikki Ducornet, Valerie Miner, Melanie Rae Thon, Paul Maliszewski.

The Constellation Martone: Tim, Amy, Ben, and Gina.

Gravity, Electromagnetic, Strong, and Weak: Theresa.